Praise for *A FALL TO GRACE* . . .

"*A Fall to Grace* is a teaching story about the healing power of love and the spiritual transformation available in the gift of intimate relationships."

Angeles Arrien, PhD
Author of *The Four-Fold Way* and *Signs of Life*

"Sandra Ingerman's intriguing novel is a rich source of conversations with wise and ancient teachers who can inspire our search for meaning in life and from whom we can learn important truths about our spiritual paths."

Tom Cowan
Author of *Fire in the Head: Shamanism & the Celtic Spirit*
and *Shamanism As a Spiritual Practice for Daily Life*

"Sandra Ingerman's novel is delightful, poignant, and sure to inspire courage in us all."

Jamie Sams
Author of *Medicine Cards*
and *The 13 Original Clan Mothers*

"Sandra Ingerman has somehow found words for the wordless. Read, and remember."

Eliot Cowan
Author of *Plant Spirit Medicine*

Also by Sandra Ingerman:

Soul Retrieval: Mending the Fragmented Self

Welcome Home: Following Your Soul's Journey Home

a Fall to Grace

a Fall to Grace

A NOVEL BY

SANDRA INGERMAN

Moon Tree Rising productions

Santa Fe, New Mexico

Published by: **Moon Tree Rising Productions**
PO Box 4757
Santa Fe, NM 87502

Edited by Barbara Moulton and Ellen Kleiner
Book design by Richard Harris
Back cover design and logo by Marilyn Hager
Back cover photo by Phil Welch

Printed in the United States of America on acid-free recycled paper

Publisher's Cataloging-in-Publication Data

Ingerman, Sandra.
    A fall to grace / by Sandra Ingerman.
    p. cm.
    ISBN 0-9655034-0-2

    I. Title.

PS3559.N4475F355 1997   813'.54
                             QB196-40550

10 9 8 7 6 5 4 3 2 1

To Woods

my true love

AM GLAD YOU ARE FOLLOWING YOUR SPIRITUAL journey." The words echo through my consciousness as if bounding off the walls of a canyon, sounding until they fade into the unknown.

I slowly take in my surroundings. I see that I am resting comfortably on a bed in a strange and beautiful hospital room. The wallpaper is vibrant with swatches of peach and swirls of spring-green. Delicate tones are flowing in from an unknown source, pulling me into a gentle peace. The light streaming into the room is also soft, and I notice pots filled with plants flowering into round, sweet-smelling blossoms.

Where am I? I ask myself. Did I die? Am I in heaven?

Glancing to my left, I see a tall, thin being moving with grace in my direction. As it draws near, I behold an androgynous face set off by a compassionate smile.

The being approaches my bed and greets me with a singsong, "Welcome." Then, as if anticipating my next question, it begins to speak. "It was not your time to go, so you were transported to a reality compatible with your spiritual pursuits."

I search my mind for recent memories . . . My life had become more challenging than usual. I was constantly exhausted by work, wondering where my career was headed, tired of the struggle to make my mark on the world, feeling lonely and isolated. I decided to go for a checkup, thinking that maybe I had one of those mysterious viruses that were attacking people, pulling the plug on their energy and will to live. I remember my absolute horror upon hearing the medical diagnosis: a tumor in the wall of my uterus. I never believed I could develop cancer—that was for others. I prided myself on my strong constitution and had worked hard to lead a life of spiritual harmony.

But I had drifted from my spiritual path, plagued by the demands of survival and of being an adult in "the real world." What was the real world anyway? It could not possibly have been what mass consciousness was defining as "real." I worked in an office with harsh fluorescent lighting, a place that did not reflect the soul of the person I thought I was. Because it had no windows, I had to depend on the clock to tell me the time of day, how hungry I was, if I was tired. I longed to see the sun hanging in the blue sky. I yearned to feel connected to the natural world, to my body, to life itself.

I guess my cancer was a wake-up call. Before I die, what regrets will I have? How will I have preferred to spend my time? Was I being given a second chance, or did I need to meet the grim reaper with my regrets?

Surgery was scheduled immediately. I said my prayers to the Creator and was wheeled by gurney into the operating room, where I was given a mild sedative. Everything began to look surreal. What a sterile environment I was in! How does anyone get better here?

Surrounding me were people dressed in spotless white gowns and masks. Who were these people? Did they care about my well-being? Did they even know who I was?

A man speaking in a monotone said that he was going to put a mask on me, that it would contain anesthesia. He told me to count backward from one hundred.

After that, all I remember is floating out of my body. What an interesting experience *that* was. Some part of my consciousness was watching from the ceiling, unconcerned about the dormant body below. I had read about this sort of out-of-body experience, and the books were right: the spirit is not emotionally attached to the body. The body is actually a container that carries the spirit from place to place. I wish I had taken better care of this container of mine. Oh, the experiences I missed because I did not let my body dance with my spirit!

While my being floated above my body, I began paying attention to the white-clad strangers, who appeared hard at work. They looked tired, drained of their life forces. Are these the healers of our time? If so, I need to rethink the concept of healing.

In the midst of ruminating on the scene below me, I became aware of a rumble. The room began to shake, and the doctors and nurses started staggering. I could smell panic. Screams filled the air. The lights swayed around me. Sterile instruments took flight, slamming into the walls. A serious earthquake was rattling the hospital where my body was being operated on to restore its state of "health."

What, I wondered, do I do now? If I reenter the body below me, I will surely die. The anesthesia mask was still covering my mouth, but I did not know how long it would continue to work, or if anyone would be left uninjured enough to help me.

While considering my options, I felt a magnetic pull on my soul. I began spiraling into space, passing through a deep, black void. This must be the place where everything began, I reasoned. Moving at lightning speed through the void, I started to experience the hum of the universe, the song of life. Then came flashes of color and faces, and feelings of well-being from my soul. Everything is perfect just as it is, I told myself.

My sense of trust kept me in what I can only describe as a state of ecstasy. I was a part of life; I was reconnected to the source; and I didn't care where I was going. I was where I needed to be. Beyond this point I remember nothing.

I GAZE UP INTO THE COMPASSIONATE, LOVING FACE OF MY attendant, who is tenderly singing, "This is the beginning of a new journey." Then I fall back into a deep sleep and move into a dream. I am floating above my body, feeling safe and cared for. Reentering the darkness of the void, I notice a figure in the distance. Drawn to it, I move in that direction and discover against the blackness around me a woman draped in midnight blue. She has a compassion different from that of my attendant. Her energy exudes not only love and caring but a demanding quality. How do I know this? I just do—I seem to be tapping into a "knowing" within me, a part of myself that has been elusive. The few times I've had knowings in my life I was unable to analyze them with my rational mind.

The woman approaches me, saying, "You must trust yourself."

Trust myself? What a foreign concept, I say silently. Aloud I ask her, "What do you mean?"

"You were wondering why your knowings, as you call them, have been so infrequent and elusive, weren't you?"

I am shocked that this robed figure is reading my mind. "Who are you?" I ask.

"I am a teacher from another world whom you have called upon for help in the next stage of your journey. More about me will be revealed as your understanding grows. Now back to you.

"You need to learn to trust yourself. These knowings deep within you arise from the part of yourself called your spirit. The spirit part of you is all-knowing and immortal. It is the aspect of you that goes beyond ego, personality, and culture. Your spirit is truth—who you really are. All the rest is simply clothing you wear that covers up your true self.

"When you die, your spirit lives on. Whenever catastrophe strikes, only the ego is affected by it. The ego, prone to views of separation, believes that something can be lost. And yes, from a personality standpoint, from a feeling standpoint, loss is possible. But you must learn to see that *you* can never be lost.

"Hence it is important to trust yourself. The more you trust yourself, the more knowings you will have—and the more your personality will unravel to reveal the true you and the beauty you truly are."

I let these words sink in, aware that what I am hearing is indisputable. Do I dare ask the figure to go on, I wonder, or do I remain asleep? The answer to this question emerges the moment I realize that a door has opened, never to close again. Although open only a crack, it is enough to propel me into the unknown.

Consumed with fear, I say to the figure, "As I listen to you, I know what you say is true. But I am afraid. Can you help me?"

"The fear that runs you is the fear of loss. And yet there is nothing to lose, for you will always have your *self*. You must see life as an adventure. Then, once you learn

that there is truly nothing to lose, you will surrender to
the adventure. It is within that place of surrender that
your path can be shown to you. It is out of that place of
surrender that your true beauty and creativity can burst
forth. No longer will the ego and personality have power
over you.

"The person you show to the world is the one you
were conditioned to be by your parents, peers, and society. This is not who you really are. Once you've surrendered to the adventure, the seed that came into this world
as you will be able to blossom into the beautiful flower it
was intended to be."

What this extraordinary woman is saying makes
sense, I tell myself. I think back on expanded states of
consciousness I experienced in childhood. I had a deep
love for nature and envisioned a life extending beyond
what the ordinary mind could see. But the "fantasy" world
I delighted in soon gave way to a perception of the "real"
world. And as it did, my wonderment started to fade. The
colors I saw in my mind lost their vibrancy. A part of me
died to the other realms until all that was left was what I
could literally see around me. I learned to take my place
in a world that from a child's point of view had no meaning. And in the process I left beauty behind.

I know I must find a way back to the magical places
I visited as a child. Yet it is no longer appropriate for me
to dwell in them full-time. How do I bring those memories into my ordinary state of being?

I ask my teacher to help me with this dilemma.

She responds, "You are simply following the path of
your soul. Yes, you have lost your way, but this, too, is part
of the learning. You would not be here had you not gathered a certain amount of life experience to draw upon.

"Now your soul has led you to me. Soon you will
meet a succession of powerful and wise beings who will

instruct you in retrieving what you call the magic in your life. Do not be deceived by the appearance of any of them; each will have a teaching for you. Learning how to receive love and truth from realms beyond the perceptions of the ordinary mind is part of the adventure."

I am filled with questions. I am also filled with great sadness. I feel as if my heart is breaking, I tell my teacher.

She asks me to stay with the feeling and follow it to its source.

I sit down. The darkness around me reflects the darkness within me. Yet just as the darkness around me is exceedingly vital, the darkness of my sadness fills me with life.

I breathe into the pain in my heart. The effort required to inhale seems immense. The effort required to live feels immense. I become lost in this feeling. While giving myself to the energy moving through my body, I pick up on another knowing: I need to detach from the feeling to see what it holds.

As I do this, I discover that the love and care I am experiencing is new to me. Until now, my heart has not been touched by another; my essence has not been seen by another. This lack of love has caused me great sadness. I vow never to go back to a life that leaves me so cold and untouched inside.

My teacher puts her hand on mine. She runs her other hand through my long dark hair. How does she know I am comforted in this way? I ask myself.

"You are beginning a new adventure," she goes on. "Take heart that the way will be shown to you. Trust in the universe. Trust in your capacity to learn not only how to survive but how to live fully. Set this as your intention when you begin your journey."

"Will I see you again?" I ask.

"Oh yes," she replies. "You can't get rid of me easily.

Even when you do not see me I will be there. And we will talk from time to time."

"Where am I? Have I gone to a different planet? Am I dreaming all this?"

"What seems to you a simple question is actually quite complex," she says. "When we dream, where are we really? When we fantasize, where are we? When we go to work, where are we?

"The answer, which will become clear later, is that 'in' and 'out' are the same. For now, don't try to figure out where you are; just give yourself over to the experience.

"You will find many ways to distract yourself from fully experiencing the upcoming journey. Avoid these temptations and stay in your center. *Don't be pulled away from your center.* It is time for me to leave you to your journey."

I am moving through space again. I want to follow my teacher's advice to give in to my experience, but too many questions are plaguing me. Where am I? What was happening to my body in the hospital room? Will I ever return, and if so, when?

My mind continues to chatter away. From its far reaches I hear, "You will find many ways to distract yourself from being fully in your experience. Remember not to get pulled from your center."

My mind, I decide, has always been a distraction to me.

"YES IT HAS!" A VOICE BOOMS.

The world around me has changed, for I am now floating on a huge white cloud. I cannot see where the voice is coming from. What I can see is a deep blue sky brimming with clouds. I recall sitting in my backyard as a child and sending a part of me up to drift with the clouds. How calming it was to be with them. How calm I am feeling now.

The next thing I know, I am seated in a classroom, surrounded by wooden desks like those I used in grade school. A man with his back to me is writing something I cannot understand on the blackboard. He is wearing a maroon cloak. As he turns around, I see that his forehead is deeply furrowed. With his long, thinning, pure white hair and white beard, he looks like the archetypal wise man. I wonder what he has to share with me.

"Well, class," he announces, "let's begin."

I look around the room and see that I am the only one here. Yet he speaks in a voice that would wake up hundreds of students in a large lecture hall.

Startling me, he shouts, *"Expand yourself!"*

In that insane moment the floor literally drops out from under me. I'm falling, out of control, through a tunnel, with no time to wonder where I am going and whether or not I'll survive. I'm hitting roots and leaves. My skin is breathing the deep, rich, dark earth in my midst. All the while a high-pitched wind whistles through the tunnel, screaming, "Let go."

Eventually I tumble out into a world unlike the one I just visited. There everything and everyone seemed to float in midair; now I am in an amazing forest.

This is a place I might have visited in my ordinary life, but it is somewhat different. How is it different? I ask myself. Although it is green, like the forests I remember, everything here is more vibrant and alive. I never saw auras, and in fact joked about people who did, but these trees have auras. The energy around them shines so brightly it appears tangible. If I were to touch this energy, it would feel like a crystal.

I get up to brush the dirt off my clothes. My face is covered with fine granules of earth, as are my hands. I look around for something to clean myself with. The ferns are huge. The trees remind me of the tall ponderosa pines I am fond of. Life is definitely present in this place—yet too alive for me to touch.

So I start brushing myself off with my hands. While whisking away the particles of soil, I note that I am somewhat in shock. The adventure is becoming a bit much for me. I want it to slow down, but I am too outside of time to mentally curb its progress.

Still partially covered with dirt, I curl up on the cool, moist earth and rest my head on a mound of pine needles. What, I wonder, did that old man mean by "expand yourself"? This is the last thought that comes to me as I fall into a deep, dreamless sleep.

I AWAKE SLOWLY. WITH MY EYES STILL CLOSED, I REVEL IN THE richness of the soil beneath me. I've forgotten how nurturing it is to simply lie on the earth, I note. I wish I had more time to do this during my busy life. I guess I could make time for it if I really want to. I need to reevaluate my priorities.

"You certainly do!" a gentle voice calls out.

Startled, I open my eyes. Standing before me is a little being. He's not a leprechaun—I've seen pictures of leprechauns, and he doesn't resemble them. Nor is he like any elf I've seen in collections of fairy tales. All I can think of calling him is a "tree man." He couldn't be more than three feet tall, and beside him stands a small doe.

They both look at me with soft brown eyes. The tree man has a glimmer in his, giving me the impression that he is laughing, despite the serious expression on his face. He is dressed in a long-tailed black coat and in pants the color of his slick brown hair.

"Who are you?" I ask.

"I'm a friend," he replies.

"Is the doe a friend, too?" I ask.

"The doe is a friend of mine," he replies.

"Oh," I comment, hardly knowing what to say.

"Are you on a search for power?" he inquires.

"I don't know. Why do you ask?"

I'm getting used to the idea that the beings I run into tend to know what is on my mind.

"You seem to have a lot of questions about power, as if you want more of it than you think you currently have."

"I guess that is true," I confess. "I have been feeling powerless. I've always felt powerless, but now it's more acute than ever, because I have been diagnosed with a life-threatening illness."

"If all the power in the universe were available to you, what would you do with it?"

"I don't know. I have never thought about it."

He looks at me with kind eyes. I feel comfortable with this little man. I know I could live here forever and be happy following him around like the doe does.

"Until you understand your connection with all that lives—and stop feeling separate from the people around you and all other life forms in the universe—it is not appropriate for you to tap into your full power. Right now your ego has hold of your power. The ego experiences itself as separate from the rest of life, and it seeks power over others. Hence the ego cannot use the power of the universe in a way that serves all."

He continues, "If you had all the power of the universe available to you, and you were feeling jealous or angry, what would the consequences be?"

The little man is right, I tell myself. What I really want is the power to heal myself and to have a good life; yet, perhaps because of my ego, I am wanting more and more power for myself.

"What is power?" I ask.

"Power is the ability to use energy," he explains. "However, what you need at the moment is knowledge. That is what you should be seeking."

"Can you give me an example of the knowledge I should be seeking? Should I go back to school for another degree?"

The wind kicks up around us, drawing my attention back to nature. Up until this time, the sun was shining through the trees and a slight morning chill was in the air. I assume that it is still morning. Or is it late afternoon? I should be able to tell the time of day by observing the sun's position in the sky, but I can't—I've become too reliant on the ticking of a clock on the wall.

Again the little man reads my mind. "How to live your life in accordance with the laws of nature—this is the kind of knowledge you should be seeking. You know that you are not separate from nature, that you cannot control nature. Control is not true power. Working *with* and living *with* is true power.

"The doctors and healers in your land seek to cure disease. But what good does it do to cure disease if they do not teach people how to live?

"If the doctors successfully remove the tumor from your body and you reengage in a life of stress and anxiety, will they have effected a cure? You might only continue to abuse the body, replacing the old illness with a new one. To move in the direction of good health and happiness you will need to see yourself as part of life. But how can you do this if you don't know the power of the sun, the earth, the moon, stars, water, wind, fire, and the ways in which they move around you, with you, and within you?"

I listen carefully to this funny-looking man with laughing eyes. I can tell he is not preaching to me: the twinkle in his eyes shows genuine concern, and his words carry an energy of pure love and wisdom. I am sure this being knows everything, and I want to know what he knows. There I go again, wanting it all, I remind myself. I have a knowing that suggests this process is going to take a great deal of patience—something I tend to run out of.

"Are you going to teach me how to live my life?" I ask.

"No, I am going to help you *remember* how to do it. All the knowledge you need is inside you. You simply have to access it."

"I often feel as if I am stumbling around in the dark."

"Then walk through the darkness. Let the strength of your spirit carry you through the void."

"I don't know how to do that."

"Well then, let's take a practice run at it, shall we?"

He steps closer and reaches for my hand. The doe follows in silence, sharing her love with me through her eyes. She has no words with which to communicate, I observe. Immediately I catch myself invalidating the importance of her presence, then I recall the gift of love that shines through her eyes. She has love to offer, I realize. What more do I seek? Isn't love enough?

We walk together in silence. The trees are so tall I cannot see the tops of them. Nor can I see the brilliance of the sun. I see only its rays streaming through the pines. The dark earth is covered with their green and brown needles. These, as well as the shade of the trees, keep the ground moist, cool, and nurturing to walk upon. My feet bounce along effortlessly.

We arrive at a clearing in the midst of which is a lagoon surrounded by earth and rocks. At the far end of the lagoon

is a waterfall. It's not a roaring waterfall I would associate with the tropics, but it's enough of a cascade to
evoke the great presence of water.

We make our way around the lagoon. Both the little tree man and the doe prance gracefully over the
rocks. Their movements are hushed. Mine, by contrast,
are loud. My footsteps are heavy; my breathing,
labored; my gait, forced and clumsy.

The little tree man looks around, his eyes twinkling.
I can see he holds all the wisdom of the universe.

We head toward the waterfall. What now, I wonder,
as the strong spray causes me to lose my balance. The
little man and the doe stop. The man turns around,
takes my hand, and glances at me with a look that says,
"It's okay." I feel a sudden rush of trust in him.

"We are going to walk behind the waterfall," he
shouts, to make his tiny voice heard over the din of the
cascade. "Just follow me."

I think about how challenging it will be to keep my
balance around all this power. Then from the back of
my mind I hear, "Distractions will pull you from your
center. Gather yourself and stay in your center."
Stopping for a moment, I try to collect myself by taking a deep breath. I can feel myself becoming centered
and mustering strength for the journey ahead.

As we near the side of the waterfall, I manage to
avoid slipping on the wet, moss-covered rocks. Again I
remind myself to keep my center. Following the little
man further, I inch my way behind the cascading
waters and, to my surprise, arrive at the opening of a
cave.

At first I am delighted by the prospect of entering
this cave, as I have never before been in one. Then my
fears start to surface. Fears often arise as I face a new
adventure, I realize. Why is that?

My imagination goes wild—bears live in caves, bats live in caves. What if some animal is in there?

The little man falls down laughing. The doe raises her nose and laughs in her own way. It is humiliating to discover that my rampant fears are known to others, but what am I to do? These beings know everything about me. There's nothing to do but breathe and try my best not to blush too profusely.

The little man stands and grabs my hand. The energy he carries inspires my confidence. In response, I stretch myself to trust a little more.

We enter the cave. The interior is how I imagined it— pitch black. The little man's hand, still in mine, is leading me through the darkness. I take comfort in his firm grip, knowing that all I need to do is follow.

Finally we reach what appears to be the back of the cave. No bears lumber up to maul us. No bats leap out and get caught in my hair. But no matter how wide open my eyes are, I can't see a thing in this kind of darkness.

The little man strikes a match and lights a lantern that is mounted on the cave wall. Reaching into his pocket, he pulls out a crystal and holds it up to the light for me. Then he turns the crystal in such a way that a rainbow of colors begins bouncing off it. But more than that, I see a brilliant light shining through it.

"Do you see the light?" he asks.

"Yes," I reply.

"A light like this lives inside you. You have your own internal light that will guide you through the darkness. Go inside yourself and try to see the glimmering light that shines there."

I shut my eyes and go inside myself the way I learned to in my relaxation classes. All of a sudden I am aware of a brilliant light in my solar plexus.

"Excellent," he says. "This is you. This is who you

truly are—beyond thought, beyond ego, beyond the impressions of others. The light that shines in you is even greater than you now perceive it to be. It has no beginning or end; its expanse is incomprehensible. Part of your journey in life is to let that light grow.

"It is important to remember that the purpose of the ego is to perceive space and time for this light inside you. But who you are is this great light, not your ego.

"As for the practice of walking through darkness—" Before completing his sentence he blows out the lantern. The light of the crystal vanishes.

"I am not going to help you leave the cave. You have many senses beyond ordinary vision. The nonordinary sense of seeing inherent in the great light within you will guide you. Let your sense of smell lead the way. Let the sensors on your skin and your knowings lead the way. I shall be at the entrance to greet you."

"But wait, I can't see!" I exclaim, ignoring the instructions the little tree has so patiently delineated. My plea is met by silence.

I take a step. Disoriented by the intensity of the darkness, I cannot tell if I have moved forward or backward. I know I am on solid earth, but neither the earth nor my body feels solid right now.

I take another step and promptly hit the cool, wet wall of the cave. I can't do this, I tell myself. But no one is going to rescue me here. Or maybe someone will. If I sit down, perhaps the little man will feel sorry for me and come get me. Perhaps this is a test of faith in the unconditional love that my new friend feels for me. No, that's not it; it sounds good, but that's just not it. I really have to do this one myself. The concept here must be, a little tough love from my friend and a lot of faith in myself.

I continue my painfully slow journey through the

cave, one trembling step after another. Then I recall the man and the doe joyfully prancing over the rocks by the lagoon, and I realize there is another way to proceed.

Breathe, I say to myself. Find your center, follow your light, I reiterate, trying to use the new knowledge I have been given.

So far, so good, I declare silently. Not simple, not smooth yet—but I'm doing pretty well. Then at the point of feeling full of myself, I trip on a rock blocking my path and fall flat on my face.

Okay, that's it, I say to myself, struggling to sit up. I've had it. I'm not moving. I am going to sit in the darkness and die here if no light appears for me to follow.

I feel the energy of the little tree man beside me. At least I can perceive that much, I note.

"What are you doing?" he asks.

"I'm sitting—what does it look like?" I say angrily.

"Are you resting?" he asks.

"No, I am not resting; I am giving up. So what do you have to say to that, O great wise one?"

He ignores my sarcasm. "The trick to moving through the darkness, dear heart, is not to sit down but to keep moving."

I feel the energy of another presence beside me. It is that of the beautiful female I first met in the void.

"You are going through an initiation," she explains.

"I don't know if I am going to live through it," I reply despondently as tears well up in my eyes. My heart holds all the pain in me: self-pity, disappointment, worry, strife, fear of failure, and on and on.

My teacher ignores this bid for sympathy. "It would not be an initiation if you thought you were going to live through it," she replies.

The little tree man and my teacher recite in concert: "Remember who you are. Remember the light that shines the way for you. Remember that the strength of your spir-it will carry you through the void." Then they are gone.

I try to collect myself enough to consider my options. How silly of me, I muse, to think I have options. Either I sit in this cave, disconnected from my body forever, or I get up and walk.

I get up. I seem always to be getting up and brushing myself off, I recall, frowning. I wish life were easier.

I start to walk, chanting to myself, "The strength of my spirit will carry me through the void." The rhythm and words of this intonation draw me away from my negative thoughts. Forgetting about my plight, I carry on. Soon I begin to smell fresh soil. I begin to hear rippling water. I begin to open my heart to joy, which replaces all the self-created pain I've been carrying. I begin to feel the strength inside me that guides me to the light at the open-ing of the cave.

How long, I wonder, did all of this take? Who knows—maybe an hour, maybe a day. All I know is it is light outside and I am walking toward that light.

Finally I emerge from the cave. The sun shines bright-ly, momentarily blinding me. I shut my eyes, then open them ever so slowly, giving them time to adjust to the illu-minated world.

I am back at the lovely lagoon, only this time the land-scape is much more vibrant. As there is no one here to greet me, I embark on a personal inventory. I note that my knees feel shaky. Actually, my entire body is trembling.

To calm my nerves and refresh my tired soul, I plunge into the lagoon. The cold water surrounds me with a puri-ty I have never felt before. I allow it to clear away the emotional debris left over from my adrenaline rush in the cave. As I float on my back, I grasp the meaning of the term "healing waters."

Kicking hard, I descend to the bottom of the pond. The water is not as murky as I expected it to be. I see an abundance of plants and many types of fish. But because I don't know enough about marine life, I am unable to identify these colorful creatures. Even so, how grateful I am to be immersed in the power of nature! Usually I am in too much of a rush for such a luxury, or too preoccupied with thoughts about what I should be doing. Here everything is different: I have no place to go and nothing to do.

I rise to the surface, flip onto my back, and gaze at the clouds as they drift through the sky. Reviewing my time in the cave, I begin to wonder what my teacher meant when she said I am going through an initiation. What is an initiation? And what am I being initiated into? The only initiations I am familiar with take place in sororities and fraternities, and I know that isn't what she was referring to.

I don't feel that I've changed, other than becoming worn out from the intensity of the experience. Still, I am glad I didn't remain on the cave floor, living out the rest of my life in darkness. Actually, I suppose I do feel a new sense of accomplishment for having overcome my paralyzing fears. I will wait and see if other feelings arise. For now, I am simply glad to be in sunlight and fresh air.

I swim across the lagoon and climb out onto a rock. There on a blanket not too far away are the little tree man and the doe. Flowing between them is an invisible transmission of love that I sense immediately. Seeing that they are having a picnic, I walk over to join them.

"Congratulations, you've made it!" the little man says in greeting. "Have a seat. You must be very hungry. Caves tend to stimulate the appetite, you know."

I take a seat on the blanket.

"So, how did it feel?" he asks, handing me a plate of strange-looking fare containing a variety of unusual plants.

"Actually, I was just thinking about that." I tell him about the chant that helped me take each step forward and about my healing swim in the waters of the lagoon.

"Each experience you have here is a piece of a puzzle about how to live your life fully," he says. "No single experience will provide the answer. Try not to analyze too much of what has happened thus far. Just allow the pieces to fall together."

Exhausted, I look around for a place to rest. I don't want to be rude to my hosts, but I can't avoid giving in to my fatigue. Besides, I feel at liberty here to take care of myself.

A mother pine tree several yards to my left invites me to lean against her. How do I know this? Through an inner voice that calls to me. Trusting that voice, I crawl to the tree. My legs feel stiff with tension. Fear, I muse, is so exhausting, so stressful on the body. Is my illness caused by fear-induced stress?

Leaning against the tree, I discover that my back, too, is stiff. The voice within instructs me to breathe in and with each exhalation to relax. Many breaths later I feel as though the tree is holding me, containing all that I have experienced, and casting no judgment. This tree, I can tell, is alive! It somehow knows me and communicates with me.

I close my eyes and lose myself in the uncanny vigor of my surroundings. I seem to be soaking up something other than beauty, something I cannot yet put my finger on.

The tree man approaches. "May I join you?"

Without opening my eyes I reply, "Certainly." I am struck by the formality of his request.

"What you are experiencing is a very important piece of the puzzle. The vitality you feel is mirroring back to you the vitality of your essence. Here you can start to learn who you really are.

"As you recognize that the tree is part of you and that you are part of the tree, a new awareness will emerge. You will be able to see that, contrary to your previous perception, there is no separation between you and the rest of life. Your mind creates separation; your fear reinforces separation; your ego feels separate. In other words, you have invented the separation. It is an illusion you live your life with.

"Now what? How are you likely to behave under the influence of this new awareness? Well, if you love yourself, then you will treat the tree and the beings of nature with love and respect. If you hold on to fear or anger, these will be the feelings reflected in your interactions, leading ulti mately to a path of disharmony and destruction."

I let the words of my wise friend sink in before responding. Finally I explain, "Sometimes I become depressed by the lack of humanity in the land I come from. The people there show no caring for other life forms, including human beings. The focus is strictly on 'me, me, me.' Surrounded by so little respect for life, I sometimes feel like I don't want to continue living. But what choice do I have?"

"The choice you have is to learn, change, and evolve. You can't save the world, but you can save yourself. The land from which you come is like a school. It has a collective lesson plan as well as individual soul lesson plans. Remember that if you are connected to all that is, your learning and growing will influence the rest of human consciousness."

"Who created this school?" I ask with a twinge of anger. "I want to speak with the person in charge."

"It's easy to fall into an existential crisis, isn't it?" the tree man replies, ignoring my little temper tantrum. "It's easy to slip into hopelessness when you forget who you are. The big picture is not for you to know at this time; when you let go of your body in death, more may be revealed to you.

For now it is important to know what you want and need from the earth experience."

"I want to be able to experience a place as exquisite as this—not one with pine trees dying from diseases caused by toxic chemicals. I want to be able to swim in water that is healing and pure, and not filled with sewage or nuclear waste."

The little man looks at me with great compassion. He is aware of my pain but does not take it on.

"I've read books about different dimensions. Have I shifted to a different dimension? Can I shift to one when I am home?"

"Yes, there are different dimensions. Actually, if you look with nonordinary eyes, you will see another side to those trees you perceive as ill. You will also see a different aspect of your body that you regard as ill. The sickness you are seeing all about you comes through eyes that have not experienced life in a harmonious way. Thus, what you see is mirrored back to you as disharmony. No, I don't think you need to travel to another dimension to see beauty and harmony. What you need to do is alter your perception of yourself as weak, helpless, and ill. You need to remember who you truly are. The states of disease mirrored back to you will then change."

"How can this be? The bottom line is that trees are dying, animals are becoming extinct, the water is so contaminated I'm afraid to drink it. What are you saying—that if I believe we are all healthy, pure, and perfect, everything will magically change? Do you think I live in la-la land?"

"I ask you not to judge what I am telling you. Simply try to understand that you are responsible for your life and your health. No doctor is going to cure you of your physical ills. No government official is going to improve your economic situation. No religious leader is going to set your mind at peace. No guru is going to save your soul. It is no longer appropriate to see yourself as a child, for there is no one to take care of you anymore. The capacity to create a good life for yourself is within *you.*

"So, step number one: See the problem. Step number two: See yourself as the solution. You singlehandedly made your way out of the darkness of the cave. Not even your mind assisted you. In fact, your mind tried to block your passage with sabotaging thoughts. What were the words you chanted—'The strength of my spirit will carry me through the void'? That is a *big knowing!* You should be very proud of yourself. Rest now, for we will soon be setting forth on a new adventure."

As I lean against the tree, my eyelids grow heavy and I drift into a dream. About me is tropical forest. The air is wet, and the limbs of the trees are heavy with deep green leaves. This place, too, feels nurturing.

My frenetic thoughts have come to a standstill. As I walk along enjoying the silence of my unusually quiet mind, I hear voices in the distance. Feeling no danger in this place, I head off in their direction.

I come to a circle of women. Sitting in the center of the circle is a young Japanese woman who appears to be in her early twenties. She is crying, and surrounding her are about fifteen women of all ages and races. They make room for me to join them. Then the Japanese woman proceeds to share her sadness.

She comes from my time in history. Apparently, I have stumbled into her dream. How interesting this is, I think to myself.

She is despondent about the wearing of makeup among older women in Western cultures. And she is horrified that elders are expected to shop and to find ways of surviving on their own. "In my culture," she says, "this season of life is a time for rejoicing, not hiding. An older woman would never wear cosmetics to hide her age; she would be proud that her face showed the wrinkles of time and experience. Nor would she be seen burdened with bags of groceries. Indeed, she would be honored and supported by her community."

The women in the circle look confused and start to chat among themselves. They speak of women "hiding their age" and "not owning their beauty."

At this point I join in the discussion. "Women where I come from not only wear makeup but have surgery to reshape portions of their bodies." No one in the circle understands this concept, so I resort to pantomime. I pull my shirt several inches from my breasts, lift my butt, tighten the skin of my face, and make snipping motions at the sides of my thighs.

The women burst into hysterical laughter.

"I myself have considered cosmetic surgery," I tell them.

The comment is met by dead silence. The oldest woman in the group stands up. Set into the aging, wrinkled skin of her face are eyes so joyful my heart wants to burst. She radiates a beauty that women of my time would sell their souls for.

She walks up to me and asks, "Do you think I am beautiful?"

"Yes, I do."

"I think I am beautiful, too," she says. "Do you think you are beautiful?"

"I'm not sure," I reply. "Sometimes I do, and other times I think I am ugly."

"Beauty is a state of being," she explains. "If you truly love and respect yourself, you will see that you are perfect as you are. You wouldn't step into a field of flowers and judge which ones are more beautiful than the others. All flowers are unique and beautiful. All animals are unique and beautiful. And all humans are unique and beautiful."

She continues, more animated now. "But humans have conscious awareness. This has brought them great trouble, because with such a trait comes the ability to think. Oh yes, thinking can be a great gift; but it can be a terrible curse as well, especially when one tries to define beauty.

"True beauty lives within us. Outer appearances mask this splendor and distract others from our reality. If you love and respect yourself, you will unleash your inner beauty. You will also become cognizant of the beauty of others.

"The culture you describe is spiritually bankrupt. What you see in the mirror is not real. People who judge you by outer appearances are not being real either."

She places her hands on my face, holding my chin in her palms. She looks deeply into my eyes as if reading my soul. Then she breaks into a wide smile, baring all her teeth. I get the message from the inside out.

The women resume their conversation, but their voices and faces fade, for my dream is transporting me to another tropical environment. I am in a one-person canoe paddling down a large river. The sun is high, and the sky strikingly clear. With no clouds blocking the intensity of the heat, I feel the sun filling me, burning brightly in my solar plexus. I am starting to understand that my outer landscape mirrors my inner one.

The river is carrying me smoothly downstream. Enjoying the journey, I begin to reflect on the notion of magic. I have learned so much recently that I wish I had the power to instantly fulfill my desires, I tell myself. I wish I had more power in my life. The word *power* catches my attention, reminding me that my little tree man friend would not approve of this line of thinking.

What does that little guy mean by "illusion"? I ask myself. Is he correct? Could I use the theory of illusion to manipulate my environment? Aha, my mind is up to its old tricks again!

All of a sudden, the water starts to swirl around me. I concentrate on paddling, for I am caught in rapids and must work hard to keep the canoe afloat. But the rapids overtake my strokes and the boat starts to curve downhill. Here we go, I tell myself.

What is that up ahead? I wonder. Surely, it's the biggest log I have ever seen. It must be at least fifty feet in diameter. The log, however, springs to life and I see it is a huge snake—an anaconda. She has three heads, all of which are looking threateningly at me. I must have disturbed her sleep, I reason, feeling nervous, as I have never been a fan of snakes.

The heads start to sway in my direction. A part of me feels revolted, yet another part is fascinated by the beauty and power of this creature. Then the anaconda swings one of her heads close to mine, baring her teeth at me.

"What do you want?" she hisses. "We are not sure what your intention is."

"I just want to paddle downriver and find my way back to my friends."

"That's not what we mean. What do you *want?* What are the powers you are calling in? You have not been clear in your intention."

"That's not true! I am a good person," I state, resenting her accusatory tone. "I haven't done anything wrong." My heart is visibly pounding outside my chest.

She repeats, "You have not been clear in your intention. You have been unaware of the powers you are calling in. Be *careful* about what you are calling in."

With this, she turns her head and begins to float gracefully away. As she leaves, she takes the rapids with her, returning the water around me to a state of peace.

I can't believe that any entity would question my intention and the powers I am calling in, I argue silently. My intention is clear: I want to live a good life and help others if I can. And I am not calling in any powers! I am outraged by the charges flung at me by this being, whoever she may be.

While I am defending myself to myself, something awakens within me. Its voice is so tiny I can barely hear it. Its counsel, however, is clear: It is advising me to look deeper into the truth of the anaconda's words.

"I will not!" I shout into the silence.

I paddle to shore. There I tie up the canoe and, spotting a real log along the riverbank, plunk down on it and begin throwing pebbles into the water. I follow the ripples as they travel outward in ever widening circles. Looking into the river, I see a reflection of clouds starting to form in the sky above. The rippling current passing over these reflections sends me into a trance.

I see a face taking shape in the water before me. It is the face of a man—a Chinese man. He has an unusually high forehead and his hair is long and white, as is his beard. Having long loved Chinese philosophy, I am excited by the idea of conversing with a Chinese teacher.

As his features become more clearly defined, the man begins to look familiar to me. Deep in my bones I feel as if I know him. Then his identity becomes evident: This man is Lao-tzu, the celebrated sixth-century B.C. Chinese philosopher.

His intense eyes stare at me through the water. He says flatly, "You have forgotten everything I taught you." A moment later he disappears.

I am shocked by this statement. How, I wonder, could I have forgotten *anything* he taught me? I know him only as an ancient teacher and have never studied his works. I am not having a very good day, I think to myself. I am certainly not responding well to criticism.

Out of the sky plunges a great golden eagle. In a flash I am caught in his huge claws. Lifting me off the ground, he says, "It is time to detach from all you are involved in. Let's go into the sky for a different perspective."

He takes me through the clouds and out into the universe, circling several planets. In the distance I see the moon and hear her calling to me. But the eagle continues his ascent.

Before long we come to another layer of clouds. Soaring through these, we arrive at a place filled with radiant buildings. It looks like a city made of crystal. As we circle the area, I am dazzled by its pastel lighting.

At last, the eagle begins his descent. He sets me down on soil composed of tiny crystal granules and stands beside me. Facing us is a large temple. This, too, is made of crystal, and bright colors are streaming from its walls. The eagle spreads his wings, and although he departs without saying good-bye, I feel his kindness and love. I'm starting to learn the art of unspoken communication, I tell myself.

Two figures dressed in white emerge from the temple. They are shaped like humans—one of each gender— though they look more like beams of light. They walk over and introduce themselves.

"I am Jonathan," says the man.

"I am Leah," says the woman.

They each take one of my hands and they say, in unison, "Come, we want to show you something."

As they lead me off, they seem to float over the terrain. I am so much denser than my two guides that I feel as if I do not belong here. At last we come to a pool fed by waterfalls of light—pastel blues, pinks, yellows, and greens—an exquisite spectacle I would associate with a palace ball. The lights spill over into the pool, which is made of clear quartz crystal dotted with amethysts all the way around.

I notice that one waterfall is larger than the others and that tucked into it is a slide. "A water slide. How amazing!" I giggle with giddiness. "Joy, joy, joy—that's what is here. Light and joy." How trite, I think, suddenly embarrassed by my emotions.

"Do you know where we are?" Leah asks, using the same gentle singsong tones as my attendant in the hospital. The voices of Jonathan and Leah are rich with love. Indeed, harmony is integrated into every part of their being.

"No," I reply. "And to be really truthful, I don't care. I rather enjoy it here."

Jonathan and Leah both laugh.

"This is where souls come to be born into bodies," says Jonathan. "Watch. Keep your eyes on the big waterfall."

I do as I am told and can hardly believe what I see. From above, crystal baskets begin cascading down the slide. Each one is filled to the brim with bouncing balls of light.

This is all too much for me. I am so lightheaded that I feel drugged.

"Pure light," Jonathan sings. "These beings are pure light."

"They are going to be born into human bodies," Leah adds. "That's why you are so elated. You are feeling the vibration of these beings of light preparing to be born into the world below."

"Boy, are they in for a shock!" The words roll out of my mouth. "Don't they know what they are headed for? Don't they know they are going to be born into a life of suffering and pain?"

Jonathan looks at me gently and says, "No. They have not forgotten who they are. They are pure light. When one remembers this, there is no suffering or pain. Light does not suffer or know pain. Light knows only light."

Leah chimes in, "In your time, your parents have forgotten their light. Your parents' parents forgot theirs too. Political upheaval in the country they came from made life very hard. Emigrating to another country and living in the throes of economic depression did not allow time for spiritual pursuits. Hence they have no memory of their origins. Bereft of easy access to these memories, they know only a sense of separation, aloneness. This feeling of isolation can manifest as fear, or often anger. The sad truth is that when you have forgotten who you are, it is hard to care for other bundles of light who come into the world.

"The earth experience," she adds, "is for remembering who you really are."

I stare at the beings of light sliding down toward the cloud tunnel leading to the world below. My throat constricts, my heart grows heavy with sadness, and my eyes fill with tears.

"Good luck!" I call out to them.

I awake with a jerk. Opening my eyes, I see that I am back at the tree, within yards of the little tree man and the doe. The forest is asleep, as are my friends. I stretch out on the ground and gaze at the sky, now glistening with billions of stars. I wonder if I've just returned from one of them. Where, I muse, did we go wrong? How did we get so messed up?

My attention is caught by the first sliver of the new moon. I feel her calling me. But I don't know how to answer.

IN THE MORNING THE LITTLE TREE MAN SPREADS OUT A BLANKET for us to sit on. Across the center of it he arranges a feast of fruits and berries. He must have gone foraging after I fell back to sleep, I tell myself.

I watch my two friends with curiosity. They seem to exhibit the same loving energy as Jonathan, Leah, and the first teacher I encountered in the ethereal worlds. Yet, like the elder in the circle of women I met in my dream, this man and doe have a light that is earthed in them.

Over a delicious breakfast I tell my friends of my nighttime adventures. Their eyes open wide as I describe my confrontation with the three-headed anaconda, my encounter with Lao-tzu, my meeting with Jonathan and Leah, and my grandstand view of new souls sliding into the world.

"I am somewhat disheartened by my experience in the crystal city," I confess to the tree man. "Although I have had fleeting feelings of pure love in my life, mostly I am caught up in feelings of separation, like those you have described to me. I am prone to fits of jealousy and bouts of anger. Usually it is a silent anger in which I refrain from yelling at the people I'm upset with—but boy, if they only knew what I was thinking. And most days I live in fear of 'what is going to get me next?' How can I remember my light while all these emotions are bubbling up inside me? How can I exhibit compassion and patience if I'm continually on the verge of agitation?

"I think the anaconda was right—I haven't been clear in my intention. My desires don't always harmonize with my thoughts. I know you are right as well, when you say it is not time for me to get fully in touch with my power. What would I do with it when I forget myself, which happens so easily?"

The little man, with a resolute expression on his face and love in his voice, says: "As long as I have known you—and that has been much longer than you think—you have wanted everything on the spot. No instant enlightenment is enduring, however. The state of consciousness you wish to attain is a life path. And the best approach to it is to develop a practice in which you can learn to step out of yourself and slowly bring your awareness back to who you are.

"When you get caught up in jealousy or anger or fear, remove yourself from the situation. Become an observer at a play—that's what life is, after all. You have a choice: You can take the actor's part so seriously that you become lost in the drama, or you can remember that you are simply acting out a script. Be patient; this perspective requires practice. For now, keep coming back to your true self.

"The same goes for what you think of as your silent anger. Actually, there is no such thing as silent anger, my dear. An unspoken emotion sends quite a reverberation into the universe, because behind every emotion is an energy. So the task is to learn to express your emotions without catapulting them through space. This is a message you will receive many times in your current journey.

"How can such a feat be accomplished? First, by acknowledging that the 'little self' is afraid. Then, by coming back to who you really are—for who you really are cannot be hurt.

"It's all very simple. You humans make life so much more complicated than it is. You look for extraordinary experiences to be awed or rescued by. But all you really need to do is remember who you are."

I recall a similar message from the first teacher I met. "I hear your words," I reply. "But I haven't yet gotten them from the inside out."

"How can you understand them if you haven't begun your practice?"

"How do I practice this?"

"Let's take a journey to your essential soul."

The tree man instructs me to lie on the blanket and close my eyes. Then in a gentle singsong voice he says, "Just concentrate on your breath. Watch your breath. As you do this, don't try to stop the activity going on in your mind; simply notice any thoughts that come up."

I follow his suggestions, relieved that I need not attempt to squelch my ever-present mind chatter. As I breathe, however, my mind begins to quiet on its own and I feel a sense of peace in my body.

"Try breathing a little deeper into your body. Draw your breath down from your lungs to the bottom of your belly. Breath is life, so let it fill every cell of your body."

I am glad to be lying down, for I'm beginning to feel lightheaded.

"While breathing, continue to notice your thoughts and feelings," he adds.

I observe that the deeper I breathe, the more I lose my sense of boundaries. I cannot differentiate between where I end and the ground begins. I feel expanded, like a balloon blown up but unable to contain the air within it.

My instructor's voice is growing faint. "I am going to clap two sticks together. The sound will help keep you focused. As I do this, I want you to repeat the following intention to yourself: 'I wish to learn who I truly am.' Don't worry about who you are stating this intention to; just put it out as a silent call to the universe."

Still in an expanded state, I sense a vision forming somewhere in the middle portion of my body. In the vision I am approaching a fire. Circling the flames are a lion, a tiger, an eagle, and a boa constrictor. Growling and hissing, they invite me to come closer. Somehow I know I have nothing to lose in advancing toward these threatening animals. I am in a state of either no fear or stupidity—I am not sure which, and the uncertainty does not bother me.

As I move forward, they take attack positions. The lion bares his teeth, draws back his ears, and swings his huge tail around as if preparing for a kill. The tiger roars fiercely, raising the hairs on my skin. The eagle swoops up with his claws extended, aiming straight for my eyes. The boa flashes his fangs and hisses. From behind, a great force comes and pushes me through the circling creatures and into the fire. I am being burned alive. My worst fear in life has come to pass!

I feel nothing as layers of skin are burned off the bone and charred to ash. I *am* nothing.

As pure consciousness, I travel to a state that precedes consciousness. This indescribable gray place exists prior to thought, prior to the Creator, prior to nothing, as nothing itself is a thought. My mind stops.

No time passes here, for nothing is present. No death exists here, because nothing has yet been born. I have no awareness of myself.

At some point I leave this place, though I have no idea how. Thought could have taken me out, but no thought was able to enter this sphere. All I know is that I am now floating in the pitch-black void and I am hearing a message: "This is where creation comes from."

Here I sense a different kind of nothingness. Nothing, yet everything, is present—no life, yet all of life.

A thought takes form: How could this be? The thought is met with a deafening silence.

Another thought: Who is this "I" floating through the void? Again no answer.

I float toward a brightly shining star. I merge with it. I am a star. Or am I?

A choir sings out: "You are a star. You are a shining light. Go to earth and shine. That is your mission. Go to earth and *shine*."

I am light—that's all I am. I have no desires, no emotions, no thoughts. Everything I need is contained in this light of pure love. It confers no judgment, no awareness of others, no consciousness of self.

As light, I continue to float through space. Then I begin to descend, whereupon an awareness starts to form—a perception of mission. With this emerges a sense of separation from the source of my being. Nothing troubling; just an awareness. First I was a light connected with everything, and now I am a single light.

Drifting downward, I spot planets around me. One of them is earth, a planet of blue water. I want to shine in this world of water, I decide, but how do I get there?

I continue my descent until I am out of the darkness and amid light-covered clouds. Here I arrive at a fountain resplendent with twinkling lights. I see that I am in a crystalline basket along with other shining lights. Although separate, we are all the same.

Gently, we are emptied out of the basket. Then we swim vigorously down the waterfall of light.

The next thing I know is I am in a tunnel—a dark tunnel. I want to get out. *I want to get out!*

Swimming through the darkness, I notice a light and begin to move toward it. The light is too bright. *The light is too bright!* It's not my light, but rather an artificial one. Wait, I cry silently, I made a mistake! I want to go back.

Lights, walls, harsh voices, and then a slap.

Where am I? I want to know. Who am I? I have no recollection of the star from which I came.

Suddenly I am aware of the clicking of sticks. They are beating rapidly. Then I hear words: "Return, return. Slowly return. Follow my voice back home. I am here waiting for you. I am here to celebrate the remembrance of who you are. I am here to welcome you home to yourself."

The voice is loving and inviting. Unable to refuse its

bidding, I follow the beautiful words back to the land of trees and sun and the little tree man with his devoted companion.

I SIT UP AND, FEELING THE BLANKET BENEATH ME, TRY TO adjust to being in my body again. My ears are ringing and my vision is unclear. The tree man, aware of my condition, gives me water to drink. Then he hands me a cup of green liquid.

"What is this?" I ask.

"It is an herbal mixture made from plants that have volunteered to help you come back."

"I don't understand this concept of plants volunteering to help me come back, but I have so much on my mind at the moment that I will have to take your word for it. Would you please remind me to ask you about this later?"

"Sure," he replies. "For now, simply drink the mixture and open yourself up to receive the gift of the plants."

I drink the mixture, and soon I am no longer between worlds or peering through a veil into my surroundings. The buzzing in my ears is gone. The fog has cleared from my eyes.

"Let's walk," the tree man says.

I get up slowly, feeling a need to hold on to my experience; the last thing I want to do is shake it loose. We then begin our walk through the forest. The ground beneath my feet feels nurturing and supportive, as if the soft earth were welcoming me home. My usual heaviness is gone. In fact, there is grace to my movements. Stepping lightly along, I feel connected to the earth and much less clumsy than before.

"You have been teaching me about separateness," I

say to the little man. "In my journey I remember being at one with the source and then falling into separation. My understanding comes from a deep place now. But please tell me more."

Without slowing down he begins, "You have been wondering time and time again how the beings you meet seem to know what you are thinking. You are captivated by telepathy, aren't you?"

"Yes," I answer. "When I was a little girl, I was intrigued by psychic phenomena. In sixth grade I wrote a paper on telepathy and found the subject fascinating."

"When I know what you are thinking, it is not because I read your mind, but rather because I am part of you. I am not a separate entity trying to understand you; I am *you experiencing yourself.* So I feel what you are feeling and I hear what you are thinking. Your thoughts are not silent to me. They are as loud as if you were thinking with your voice.

"You have been told that you didn't speak until you were nearly four years old. Well, all that time you *were* speaking. You were hearing what people said to you and responding in what you might call an inaudible way. But the density of those around you blocked their capacity to hear your words. As a result you shed this mode of aware-ness and adopted that of the adults around you.

"In your culture silent communication and invisible worlds are no longer accepted. A major portion of con-sciousness has been cut off. But the point I want to make now is that we are all one, or one mind. With an under-standing of the one mind, it is easy to hear the thoughts of others.

"You keep wondering where you are. You started in a hospital room in your ordinary world and believe you have traveled to many different places. Where are these places? If you'll recall, the first teacher you met said that 'in' and 'out' are the same." He stops to give me a chance to recall her teachings.

"Yes, I remember that. And I do question where I am. Did I travel out to another world? Am I dreaming?"

"Whether you traveled outside yourself or inside yourself, the effect is the same. As above, so below—as within, so without—this teaching is popular among the metaphysicians of your time. There is no separation. So I am outside of you; and yes, I am inside you; and yes, I am you. Don't you see that these are all the same?"

"I should be confused by what you are saying, but I understand it—probably because of the powerful journey you led me on. I just don't know what to do with it. Please continue."

"Okay," he says. "Now let us look at the inverse of this perspective. Let's look at allergies."

"Allergies?" I am shocked that he would allow something so mundane to enter our conversation.

"You consider yourself a victim of allergies, don't you?"

"Yes." I am still waiting to see what this has to do with the one mind.

"When you have an allergic reaction, your brain tells your body that it is under attack by an outside agent. Perceiving the body to be in danger, the brain triggers the release of histamines to fight off the presumed invader. Hence the body goes to war with an enemy that is really not an enemy. This is an extreme response to perceiving oneself as separate. Everything outside is seen as an enemy against which to wage war.

"If you could merge with the apparent enemy and see that it is life itself, there would be no threat. With no threat, there would be no need to wage war and a sense of harmony would ensue."

"If this is true," I reply, "then the same concept would

hold true for my cancer. If I could see my tumor as part of me and not as an enemy, it would not threaten my well-being. Could I carry on a conversation with my tumor?"

"Yes, you could, if you had cancer."

"But I do. That's how I got here. I was undergoing surgery to remove a cancerous tumor when all of a sudden an earthquake sent me into your world, or my world, or whatever," I say, exasperated.

"You don't have cancer," he insists. "The doctors made a mistake. When you come out of surgery, you will be told there was no tumor in your body. The surgeon will apologize profusely for the error."

"How do you know this?" I ask excitedly.

"Because you told me. You knew it all along. The part of you that extends beyond personality has always known it; you just don't know how to access that part of you yet. This is a tremendous amount of information to absorb at once. Do you want me to stop?"

I look at the clear blue sky. My head does feel quite full. Still, I want to know more. I want to get to the end of the story.

Again the little man knows my thoughts. "There is no end to the story. As soon as you think there is an end, you will discover a new beginning. There is no place to get to, my dear. There is only the journey.

"Why don't we take a short break. Let's walk back to the lagoon in silence. There's someone I want you to meet."

We begin walking, with the doe in the rear. Thoughts are swimming around in my head—separation, telepathy, allergies. How complex and simple it all seems.

Soon the image of Lao-tzu enters my mind. Gazing into his eyes, I see a beautiful long river. The river flows into a waterfall. The waterfall returns the water to its source, the mighty ocean.

This vision ends as quickly as it began. A part of me, I realize, has opened up, and thoughts, feelings, and rememberings of all kinds are surfacing.

WE REACH THE LAGOON. TURNING AROUND, I NOTICE THE doe has disappeared. I am alone with the tree man for the first time since my emergence from the cave.

"Come over to the water with me," he urges. "Kneel down and look at your reflection in the pond."

I do as he says and study my face in the still, clear water.

"Now dive through your reflection and follow me," he declares, jumping into the water.

Without questioning, I dive through the image of my face and descend into a steep tunnel. Breathing under-water comes naturally as I swim through the passageway. Ahead of me I see a light. Uh-oh, another light at the end of a tunnel, I think to myself, recalling my trauma of being born into the world.

Following the tree man, I swim out into a new realm. I am now on foot in a beautiful green meadow. The sun is shining, and the wind is blowing the high grasses. Scattered about us are tall wildflowers. This is a place of beauty, magic, and untouched nature.

Something begins moving rapidly toward us. The ground vibrates. The swaying grasses rustle. They are so high I cannot see what is approaching. I can barely see the little tree man.

Finally, the movement slows and the meadow returns to its natural vibration. A new energy is coming to join us. I wonder what, or who, it could be.

Suddenly a tiger emerges from the meadow to greet

us. A tiger welcoming us, I think to myself. I must be dreaming.

As the animal draws closer, I notice something unusual about him: he has one blue eye and one green eye. He bounds up to me and gazes into *my* eyes. "Stroke my head," he says silently.

In my wildest imagination I never thought of myself petting a great cat like the one standing before me. I stroke the top of his head, surprised at the softness and moistness of his fur. With my other hand I stroke the warm, moist fur on his back. What a sense of power I feel from the vibration of his body. It's quite overwhelming.

Silently he instructs us to get on his back. The tree man climbs up behind the great creature's head, then I climb up behind him. He holds on to the skin around the tiger's neck. I hold on to my dear friend's body.

The tiger begins to run through the meadow. As we fly along, the wind caresses my face, taking away the thoughts that have filled my mind. The grasses and flowers bend before us in welcome. Yellow, red, and purple flower heads seem to dance against the greens of the meadow and the blue sky overhead.

As we continue on our journey, I see the faint outlines of a mountain range in the distance. It will probably take us days to reach it, I calculate, unaware of how swiftly the tiger is moving. In fact, we are there in no time at all. The mountain before us is small, compared with those I am familiar with. And it is treeless, composed solely of brown-black earth and rocks.

As we draw closer, I notice an opening in the side of the mountain. Oh, no, I tell myself, not another cave. I want to be done with darkness for a while.

"Relax," says the tree man. "We are going to a special place."

The tiger stops directly in front of the opening. The

little man jumps off, whereupon the tiger kneels to let me down. Because we have been riding for quite some time, it takes me a while to get a sense of my legs. Still a bit wobbly, I follow the tiger and the tree man to the mouth of the cave which, unlike the previous one, is wide enough to let in the outside light.

We step inside. I am amazed by the spectacle before me. The ceiling and walls are covered with huge crystals of clear quartz, amethyst, green fluorite, and yellow and pink topaz. Lining the crystals are rubies, emeralds, and fool's gold. This is nothing short of a mineralogist's dream, I muse. But for now it is my dream to be inside this place of power. The cave is shallow, and its earthen floor grounds me as I stand within the energy fields of all these crystals.

"I told you I was taking you to a special place," the tree man says. "Now sit down on the earth, close your eyes, and soak up the light from the crystals. This is a healing cave, and it is a place you can travel to whenever you feel the need for well-being. Just let the light flow around you and through you. This light will help you remember your own light."

I follow his instructions, feeling the light throughout my body. Instantly I experience a soothing calmness as a gentle energy flows through the air about me and through the cool, living soil beneath me.

When I open my eyes, I see that my friends have built a small, quietly warming fire in the center of the cave. I am surrounded by great power—from the crystals, the fire, the tiger, the tree man, and the earth beneath me. Yet this power is gentle, unlike the abusive, controlling, dominating, and dangerous forms of power I am accustomed to. The softness of this power is delightful.

The tiger stretches out on the ground, resting his

head on his huge forelegs. The tree man sits staring into the flames. I am cross-legged, gazing back and forth at my friends, the crystals, and the fire.

The little man is the first to speak. "Are you aware of the great disappointment you feel in life?"

"I am aware of many disappointments," I respond.

"Do you believe that the people around you see you for who you are?"

"Oh, *that* disappointment. No, I have never felt seen by the people around me. One of my goals is to find people who *can* see me for who I truly am. And now, thanks to your help, I know who I truly am. Maybe with the change in my awareness I will be able to find individuals who will see me."

"You might be disappointed in your endeavors. Because the humans of your time perceive themselves as separate from the rest of life, they tend to project their thoughts and feelings onto others. This way they can see aspects of themselves mirrored back to them.

"Different people mirror back different qualities. One might reflect anger, giving the impression that the person himself is angry. Another might reflect sadness. Still others will sit before a great spiritual master and have mirrored back to them their own light or the loving heart that dwells within them.

"The problem occurs when one is unaware of the dynamics of projection and attributes the mirrored qualities to individuals in the environment. A woman repulsed by her partner's anger, for example, may not see that it is *her* anger she is repulsed by. She may consequently judge her partner in lieu of owning the projection. This dangerous state of mind is prevalent in your time.

"Here's another example. A man who studies with a wise, loving teacher may ascribe to his mentor a love that in fact lives within him. False dependencies of this sort lead to unfortunate illusions.

"Serious misunderstandings arise when one casts onto another what one likes or dislikes about oneself. There is no way to be in right relationship with oneself or another while attached to these projections."

"Are you saying that no one will ever see me for who I am?" I ask.

"Anyone looking through the eyes of ego and personality will be seeing qualities of himself in you."

"How absolutely depressing."

"It doesn't have to be. Knowing who you are is really all that matters."

"But for me there is loneliness in that."

"As you begin to acknowledge your projections and claim your own light, you will not feel this loneliness."

"How can you be so sure?"

"Because you told me with your inner wisdom."

After a pause, he continues. "All humans want their beauty to be seen. All humans want to be loved. The first step is to love yourself. And the way to do that is by remembering your light. Whenever you feel separate from others, remember that the separation is an illusion of the mind."

"While practicing this awareness you speak of, how am I supposed to live my life? I have to get up and go to work. I have to be able to function in traffic, at the supermarket, at the bank. If I start to envision myself as a floating light, how will I get anything done? How will I keep myself out of a mental institution?"

"Your point is well taken. The body is a container for the spirit. The more your spiritual awareness grows, the stronger your container will need to be. As you bring this new awareness of yourself into your ordinary life, it is essential to take care of your body, because it is your body that holds you."

"Do I have to gain weight and become a bigger container?" I ask in horror.

"No," he giggles, "you have to become strong. You won't want to fry any fuses on the inside."

With that, we both break into laughter.

All this time the tiger has been gazing into the fire, seemingly uninterested in our philosophical discussion. "I don't suppose the tiger has something to teach me about becoming strong in my body." I laugh out the words.

"You have a great laugh," says the little man. "You should laugh more often."

THE THREE OF US LEAVE THE CAVE TOGETHER. ONCE OUTside, the tree man and I mount the tiger, who takes us back to the meadow.

I feel lighthearted as we slide off the animal's back. Right away, he roars and begins chasing us. We all run in circles through the tall grass, chasing one another. The tiger dashes up to me and sticks his head nearly in my face, baring his teeth; then he roars. I take my own cat stance, baring my teeth, hissing, and pawing at his face. He paws at mine in return, whereupon we roll on the ground together, playfully growling and hissing at each other.

There is a message in this play, I realize, for I am learning to stand in my own power. I then flash on the words of the tree man: What matters is the journey, not the end of the story. I stop myself from drawing conclusions, aware that the tiger will be in my life for quite a while.

Tired out, I lie in the soft grasses, trying to catch my breath. I am a bit out of shape, I admit to myself. And it's been a long time since I have played. My life has become so serious with work, survival, and politics.

Romping with the tiger has relieved me of one more layer of tension, reminding me of the need to change my priorities. I have forgotten who I am, how healing nature can be, even how to laugh. These cornerstones of existence lie buried beneath mounds of paperwork. Thinking of the duties that await me, I become overwhelmed by the prospect of returning to my ordinary life.

"Don't distract yourself from the experience at hand," cautions the tree man, having heard my thoughts once again. "Stay with your experience. As one of your previous teachers says, Worry takes you into the past or the future, and never lets you deal with the present. Bring your attention back to the present each time you catch yourself wandering off."

"Does this mean I don't have to look at my past?" I inquire.

"No, your past can provide a helpful perspective. From this vantage point you can see how your earlier life experiences influence your current decisions and patterns. This is very important work. One who can see clearly what has been running her life has the capacity to make new choices. To dwell on the past without raising your awareness, on the other hand, may cause you to re-create old painful situations over and over again. You have the power to change your life, remember?"

He doesn't wait for my response. "There are times for contemplating the past and times for staying in the moment. When delving into the past or future to escape the present, try to find your way back so that you can observe the feelings arising in the here and now."

"I wonder why I avoid the present so much."

"Being in the present brings up feelings you may prefer to ignore. Being in the present also requires you to be fully alive in the moment, and you are not always willing to be alive. You seem to be avoiding life."

"Life is often difficult for me. I don't feel comfortable in my body. I'm unsure of myself around other people. In fact, you are the only individual I have been truly comfortable around. I admit I have not always appreciated my life. I have considered suicide many times."

The tree man looks at me with a serious expression I have not seen before, and the twinkle fades from his big brown eyes. "You must decide whether or not you want to be in this life. You cannot continue to live with one foot in the world of death—not with all you are learning here. The effects will be devastating. Life will only become worse for you if you cannot step fully into the knowledge you are acquiring. You will become no more than another of the walking dead in your world.

"Let us not go any further in this journey until you decide whether you want to live or die."

Suddenly everything goes black. I am floating in the void again, but it is not the void I visited previously. The void I was in before was filled with life; now I am between life and death. The energy here is flat.

I AM BEING PULLED BACKWARD THROUGH SOME MYSTERIOUS veil between the worlds. I hear a loud popping in my ears. Opening my eyes, I see I am in the operating room.

Confusion abounds. Gloves, scalpels, and IV tubes lay helter-skelter about the room. The fluorescent lights are blinking on and off in response to surges of electricity. The doctors' and nurses' eyes freeze with terror. The surgeon and attendants realize what has happened.

I watch from the ceiling as they reassemble around my body. What will happen to me? I ask silently. Can they save my life? Do I want to live?

Shock and fear drive me back into the void. "Help me decide to live," I call out. "Help me know how to do this!"

I am floating in the void, convinced that I am having a heart attack. I can't breathe. My chest is constricted. The life force is being sucked out of my body. "Help me!" I cry.

"I am here," says someone softly. I open my eyes and see a woman kneeling beside my body.

"Who are you?"

"In your world I am known as the Virgin of Guadalupe. Here I am your mother who is willing to help you. Please close your eyes."

Our Lady of Guadalupe puts her hands on my heart. "I have heard your call many times. The energy I contain lives within you. Let me help you remember."

Feeling her hands over my heart, I begin to breathe more easily. The calm and peace that has left me returns.

"When I place my hands on a person in a healing way," she explains, "I am not channeling healing energy in from the outside; I am helping the person remember the source of all healing, which resides within. I am helping you heal from the inside out. That is what you need right now. Remember the source of life that is in you."

Her hands remain in place a while longer, then she quietly departs, leaving the imprint of her love on me. I feel grace—something I've often prayed for without knowing what it was. Now I know what grace is.

Returning to the hospital room, I observe the confusion. The surgeon appears uncertain about how to resume the operation; he is in shock. The anesthesiologist takes a seat behind the operating table and attempts to regain his composure. He asks a nurse to wipe the sweat from his forehead, as already it is dripping into his eyes.

This time I am watching from a corner of the room. I am not in a state of fear; in fact, I feel relatively calm as I survey the activity taking place around my body. The surgeon lifts his hands, then stops. I am hemorrhaging. He cannot find where the blood is coming from. The events surrounding the earthquake have seriously shaken his ability to concentrate.

A form appears behind him. It is Our Lady of Guadalupe. No one except me seems to be aware of her presence. She gently merges her hands with the surgeon's, guiding his fingers to the damage that has caused the bleeding. The terror in his eyes begins to fade. Reading his thoughts, I can see that he attributes his renewed concentration to the adrenaline pumping through his body.

At this point Our Lady of Guadalupe steps over to the assisting nurse and places a hand on each of her shoulders. The nurse's face relaxes as she searches for the proper instruments to hand to the doctor. Our Lady then works her way around to the anesthesiologist and places her hands on his forehead. A smile begins to form on his lips.

The operating table, the doctors, and the nurses turn fuzzy as I once again drift from the room. My consciousness shifts to a light-filled tunnel. The light here seems warm and welcoming, in sharp contrast to the cold fluorescent lamps in the room. I allow myself to be pulled forward by it. Floating through the tunnel, I feel at peace. I know that my body is in good hands and that I will have a physical container to reenter. Although I am grateful to have been traveling through many wonderful worlds, I know that when the time is right I will want to return to my body.

THE TUNNEL ENDS, LEAVING ME IN A NEW LANDSCAPE. I AM standing on soil that feels less powerful than that of other lands I have visited. Facing me is a gray, murky lake. The sky is dark with clouds, and the air so wet and clammy that I feel as if bugs are crawling on my skin.

I glance around and see people approaching. Looking more closely, I discover that they are not ordinary people but rather an army of skeletons carrying metal shields. Skeletons! I tell myself, aghast. I must find a place to hide. But not a tree is in sight. I notice rocks in the distance, though I'd never get to them in time. If I wish hard enough, I tell myself, perhaps I can disappear from this place.

The clanking of armor over bones jolts me to my senses. I will have to stand and face them, I realize. Besides, maybe they are just passing through. Suddenly I feel at a loss, for I don't know the rules here. There is something recognizable about tigers that play with humans, tree men who hold all the wisdom of the universe, trapdoors in classrooms, even beautiful women leading me on; but nothing about this place is familiar to me. I don't know how to behave.

By the time my mind stops chattering, the skeleton troops have halted—in formation, with their shields before them. The head skeleton, carrying a shield decorated with a two-headed phoenix, walks up to me. He puts his hand on my shoulder. His bony fingers are cold, but I know by his touch that I am safe.

He has no words for me. He simply turns around and with a bony index finger points across the lake. He then points to a long rowboat on the shore. I know I am supposed to accompany him to the boat. He leads; I follow; the army marches behind me in perfect formation.

A sadness wells up in my heart, though I'm not sure why. Perhaps because there's no play in this world, no twinkle in the skeleton's eyes to comfort me, no sun overhead. There is no joy here. That's it, I tell myself, I'm sad because there is no joy in my midst.

Here I have no choice but to stay in the present. I cannot return to the past, and I have no idea where I am going. All I can do is experience the heaviness in my heart and take my place in the boat.

One of the skeletons pushes the craft into the lake and holds it for the rest of us to board. The head skeleton goes in first and stands while I step in. Feeling the boat move beneath me, I stumble. If ever I need to stay in my center, it will be on this journey, I say silently, steadying myself.

The skeleton points to a seat draped with a burgundy cloak, and I make my way toward it. He walks behind me, picks up the cloak, wraps it around me, and gently pushes me onto the seat. The rest of the skeletons pile in and set their shields at their feet.

With the head skeleton standing up front, holding his phoenix high against his chest, the army of skeletons begins to row. We inch our way through the fog. This is not going to be a fast journey, I mutter to myself, noticing the effort that is required to propel the craft through the thick, murky water. In places it seems as though the boat wants to circle around and return to shore.

The skeletons row on, pulling us through the heavy tide. The "lake," it turns out, is an immense body of water. The sky, still a dreary gray-black, is bare of birds. Not a sign of life appears below us either, although the water is too polluted for me to know for sure. I wonder if by not deciding to live fully I am doomed to ride out my existence on thin lifeless sea.

On the horizon I spot an island. The crew rows toward it. As we draw nearer, one of the skeletons hops into the water, grabs a rope tied to the front of the boat, and begins pulling us to shore. Then several more skeletons jump out and join in the effort, pushing from the rear.

The head skeleton, still carrying his phoenix shield, leaps out and wades through the water to the island. I remain seated until the boat is securely on land. While disembarking, I notice that the air here smells stale. To avoid taking it in too deeply, I limit myself to shallow breaths, which slows the energy flow in my body. I am tired from the trip. I am tired from the heavy mustiness of the air. I am just plain tired.

The army of skeletons stays with the boat while the head skeleton points in front of us and begins to walk. I know from his index finger that I am supposed to follow. We proceed to a huge gate. To my horror, bones and skulls are hanging from its wrought-iron lattices. Facing the gate, he points again. I wait for him to lead, but he doesn't budge—he just looks at me and points at the gate. He seems to want me to continue on my own.

"There is no way I am going through that gate alone,"
I announce, speaking aloud for the first time since my
meeting with the skeletons. The words boomerang off the
surrounding rocks, for there is no life here to absorb
them.

The skeleton continues to point at the gate. I quickly
consider my options. No way could I swim back to our
starting point; the distance is too great, and the water too
disgusting to set foot in. I could scream, but then I'd yell
for an eternity without being rescued. If I were truly in
danger, I reason, someone would come. Or is this another initiation experience—one that I may *not* live through?

The skeleton, unshakable in his mission, continues to
point. Finally I realize from a place of hopelessness and
despair that I have no choice but to walk through the gate
and face my fear.

I pull the burgundy cloak over my shoulders. Heavy
with moisture from the air, it imparts comfort, like the
blanket I once wrapped around my body at night. Then
leaving the skeletons behind, I begin my death march
through the gate. My head is down, my gait slow and
heavy. Even though I am hardly breathing, my heart is
beating rapidly with fear.

I open the gate, letting it swing shut behind me. Here
the land, like the sky, is gray. Canyons of gray rocks cut
steeply through the gray, lifeless soil. The ashen sky is
forbidding.

While walking along, I come upon thousands of people moving very slowly in a circle. They, too, are gray and
are dressed in gray cloaks. Aware that there is no light
here to mirror back my essence, I assume that they are
the walking dead. With their heads down, they shuffle in
formation, never lifting their feet from the ground. I am
riddled with questions: How long have they been here?
How long will they be here? What is this place? I can only

conclude that it is a living hell, for these shuffling beings are neither alive nor dead.

I join the circle, turning my head slowly to gaze upon the burgundy cloak covering my shoulders. It has lost its color and is now gray. Looking at my hands, I see that they are gray as well. I lower my head and begin shuffling. Having given in to despair, I am consoled by aligning myself with this lifeless pace.

An awareness begins to dawn in my dulled mind: I have a mission here, and it is not to shuffle but rather to find something. As I ponder my situation, I hear a voice.

"Help. Help me." The plea is devoid of emotion.

Find the voice, I say to myself.

"Help me. Please help me." Again the voice is lifeless.

I slowly lift my head. The despair I feel weighs so heavily upon me that all movement is painfully arduous. Just as slowly, I turn my head to see where the voice is coming from. One of the shuffling forms catches my attention. Step by step I cross the circle, cutting off some of the figures to my right. They don't seem to care; they stop momentarily, then move on. I follow a pull on my solar plexus, leading me toward the being who seems to be calling.

I spot the figure and walk beside it for a while. Without varying my gait, I lift off the hood of the one next to me. Stopping in horror, I scream into the silence, "It is me! This being is me! This plea for help is coming from *me*."

I take the hand of the one beside me, for I do not want to lose her. Holding her hand, I continue to shuffle along, my heart beating rapidly. I am radically out of place here, I tell myself. Although I feel sucked dry, I know that I have a hundred times more life force than anyone around me and that I must leave before I die, too.

Quickening my shuffle, I leave the circle with my other self in hand. The heaviness in the air, the gloominess of the place, and the lifelessness of my other self slow me down. I struggle to speed up. My intention helps carry me to the gate of this living hell.

Once on the other side, I am greeted by the skeleton. I drop to the ground, drained by the lack of fresh air. The skeleton lifts me up by the arm and points to the waiting boat. Then he picks up the other part of me and carries her in his arms. We enter the boat, where I collapse onto a seat. The skeletons push the craft into the sea and climb aboard. The head skeleton, with his shield at his feet, takes a seat, still holding the piece of me I have retrieved from this place of living death. As soon as the rowing begins, I lose consciousness.

When I open my eyes, I see the tiger and the tree man at my side in the meadow. Beside them stands the skeleton holding my other self. He bends down and extends his arms toward the tree man, who takes the lifeless part of me. He sets her on the ground, brushes his hands over her, and breathes over her until her chest begins to heave with the force of life. The tree man then places a small quartz crystal inside her heart. Next he lifts her, and as he does so, she transforms into a ball of light, which he blows into my heart. Joy and peace return to me.

I sit up with a start.

"Welcome home," the tree man says.

He is always welcoming me home from my adventures, I note. "What the hell just happened?" I ask him.

"Before you could decide between life and death, a piece of work had to be completed. Each time in your life when you wished yourself dead, you sent a piece of yourself to the Land of the Dead. A major part of your life essence, or soul, has been waiting there to be rescued. You found the piece that needed retrieving, and I blew it back into your heart.

"People often send away pieces of their souls. Yet always these missing parts wait to be recovered. The cause of soul loss can be trauma, illness, shock, abuse, or grief. This is all you need to know for now. Later you will learn more.

"What is important is that you are back home in one piece. Now you can opt for life over death and get on with your existence. But you must choose. And you must choose now. If you want to live, state it to those who witness you here. If you want to die, let us know so we can arrange for that."

I look at the little man, the tiger, and the skeleton, each of whom is awaiting my decision in the most serious manner possible. I inspect the ground. I investigate the sky. I know that whatever I say will have significant consequences. If I choose to die, my future is certain; if I choose to live, it is unknown. But the little tree man is right, I can no longer continue living between worlds. I need to have both feet in one realm.

Again I look at my friends. Then I gaze into the waiting universe and shout, *"I choose to live!"*

Even the skeleton seems happy.

THE NEXT FEW DAYS ENTAIL NOTHING BUT PLAY. I WATCH THE sun, high in the sky, giving way to the moon and the night. I stop counting the passing hours and give in to the moment.

The skeleton, meanwhile, has returned to his army. I've grown fond of him and will miss him. The doe, I'm told, is at her home by the lagoon. The tree man, the tiger, and I spend our time romping in the meadow. We speak of nothing important and merely act silly.

In the midst of our antics the tiger has become my coach. He teaches me how to stalk as we take turns stealthily pursuing each other through the grasses. He teaches me how to gather the energy roaring up inside me and how to sound it out into the world. He shows me how to be passive yet acutely attuned to my surroundings. I am awed by his wordless grace, beauty, and power.

Then the tree man asks me to go foraging with him. Up to this point he has been gathering food on his own, appearing out of the blue with meals for me. Now we go off together, leaving the meadow behind and arriving at a hillside where the grass is not so tall and allows for the growth of several varieties of plants.

"The plants volunteer their lives for us," he says.

My hunch is that he is picking up where we left off back at the lagoon, only now I am ready to listen. "Volunteer their lives for us? I don't understand."

He continues, "Do you know anything about hunting in the old way—not for sport, but for survival? Have you ever met anyone who hunts in this way?"

"I once met a man who did; he thought he came from a different time. I've also read books about this form of hunting. But most of the hunters I know view it as a sport."

"Are you familiar with the idea that an animal knows when it is about to be killed and volunteers its life?"

"Vaguely," I answer. "I once became a vegetarian because I thought I shouldn't eat anything I couldn't kill on my own. I didn't feel good going into stores and buying meat that was all packaged up."

"What happened?"

"I got hungry. So after a few months I went back to the stores and bought neatly packaged kill again. I don't think these animals volunteered their lives for me, but on a gut level I know what you mean."

"Think of plants," he goes on. "Plants are special beings that do volunteer their energy for nourishment and healing. If you are sick, you can actually find the spirit of a plant willing to provide a cure. Many medicines are made out of plants, but when they are processed their spiritual offerings are lost. What is important to remember is not only that a plant has biochemical components but that it has a spirit just like you do. If a plant volunteers to merge its spirit with yours for healing, the power of the healing will be that much greater.

"All beings are alive. All life is sacred. This is a concept most people in your time have forgotten. When human beings were dependent on nature for survival, their behavior was more interdependent. But with modern technology humanity, living in the illusion that it has power over nature, has lost its understanding of the interdependence of all life. We're back to that issue of separation again, but in a different form. People believe that nature serves them by furnishing unlimited resources and that they do not in turn serve nature."

"People in my time are arrogant. Is this what you are saying?"

"Arrogant and also childlike. They think that all of life exists only for them and that everything they want will always be available, that no resource will ever be depleted. When one recognizes the sacredness of all life and learns to live in harmony with it, whatever is needed *will* be provided. But the attitude of 'abuse and conquer without consequence' reflects a state of ignorance. Life on earth is based on harmony; disharmony creates scarcity, which generates disease. That is one of the primary issues facing you at this time.

"What I really want to do is help you remember how to live in harmony. So let's gather lunch. Begin by closing your eyes halfway—just enough to see where you are going. Then as you walk through the vegetation, notice any attraction you may feel to a particular plant. Sit down by it, and I will come show you the next step."

I take a deep breath and, with my eyes slightly closed, begin walking among the plants. I sense different energies coming toward me. Near some plants, I feel myself pushed away; near others, I feel nothing. Suddenly I feel a plant pulling at me like a magnet. I sit down beside a tall green plant with beautiful yellow flowers popping out the top of its stem.

The tree man comes and sits beside me. "Close your eyes," he tells me. "Take a few breaths and settle into your center. What are you experiencing as you do this?"

"I feel and see the light that lives inside me. I experience myself as light, not as a body. It's a wonderful feeling."

"Now allow the light of who you are to merge with the spirit of the plant next to you. Don't think about it—just hold the intention to do it."

I feel myself becoming one with the plant. A loving, nurturing energy swirls about inside me, and I meet it with my light, exchanging essence for essence. I am in union with this plant and no longer know what is me and what is the plant. This, I conclude, must be the sense of oneness the little man keeps talking about.

"Now pull your energy from this plant enough to be able to speak with it, remembering as you do that you are still part of the plant and the plant is still part of you. Ask if it will share its life with you. Ask what it has to give you."

I ask these questions, thrilled to be actually talking to a plant.

The green and yellow plant replies: "As you receive my spirit into yours, I will heal your anxiety and return your essence to its original calmness. I am happy to do this for you, but you must be willing to receive the gift. Eat me, and as you do, open yourself fully to receive the healing. Do not eat unconsciously—pay attention to the energy you are taking in and merging with."

I think back to my customary eating habits. Boy, do I go unconscious, I tell myself. Rarely do I have a clue about what I am eating. I am usually shoveling whatever I can find into my mouth because I've waited too long and my blood sugar has dropped to dangerous levels. Or I am daydreaming, or working, or talking a mile a minute as I chew. It will be a new experience to open myself to nurturing. I wish someone had taught me this before.

The little man interrupts my reverie. "Following your breath, bring your awareness back into your body, and when you are ready, open your eyes."

He waits for me to open my eyes. "Now wasn't that simple?" he asks.

"How do I know I wasn't making it up?"

"Notice how you feel after eating the plant. That will be the true test."

The tree man shows me how to pick the parts that are best to eat, leaving enough for the plant to regenerate itself. I place the pieces in the palm of my hand and bow to the plant, silently expressing gratitude for this gift.

The little man then leads me to another area on the hillside, where I sit in silence and eat the plant. While swallowing the fresh green leaves, I sense a wave of peacefulness washing over me.

"There are laws of nature that human beings must abide by," the little tree man adds as we make our way back to the meadow. "They may think they are above the law, but in reality we are all accountable to nature and its laws. We are each a part of life, and not separate from it.

"And so you must continue finding food sources that are nurturing. Even if you buy food in a store, you can take it home and merge with it. Find out how it will nurture you. If you discover that what you bought will not energize you, consider returning it to the earth rather than taking it inside you. You will slowly learn which foods are enhancing and which ones are destructive."

"I am not going to ask about my sugar habit," I remark as we begin our return to the meadow.

The tree man looks at me and laughs.

"Will I be able to learn more about plants and their healing abilities?"

"If you choose to, but it is not your life's work."

"What do you mean by my 'life's work'? I thought my mission was to shine."

"Earth is a planet of manifestation. Shining your light means giving expression to your creativity. It does not mean sitting on a bench in a garden and beaming at passersby. That could be someone's life mission, but it is not yours. Yours is to express the beauty of your soul in the world."

"How do I do this?"

"By following your passion."

"Please elaborate."

"You must do what brings you passion, fills your heart with joy, and infuses your life with meaning. If you don't follow your passion, your life may become barren and meaningless, leaving empty spaces within you. Empty spaces provide breeding grounds for bacteria, viruses, and other life forms that can take up residence in the body. They begin to colonize when they have more desire for life than you do. Then they feed upon your body, and you become their container.

"If you follow your passion, however, you will be full of yourself. The internal microorganisms will then be content to live in harmony with you, allowing you to remain physically and emotionally healthy. When you begin doing what has meaning for you, you will love your life. Of course, there will still be issues to deal with, up-and-down cycles like the ebb and flow of the ocean's tides, but that is a topic for another discussion. For now, please remember that one of your adventures in life is to discover the path that makes your heart feel full."

By this time we are back at the meadow. The tiger is lying in the grass, soaking up the warm rays of the sun. Aware of our presence, he stretches every part of his body. Imagining how good this must feel, I try to follow his example, but I am unable to access all the parts of my body, and I end up feeling tight.

The tiger watches me and, with his different-colored eyes, seems to say, You must learn how to loosen up, woman!

Yes, I must, I admit silently.

"Are you up for another walk?" asks the tree man.

"Sure, the air is beautiful and I feel rested. I'd like nothing more than to keep moving with the energy of the plant I've eaten."

The tiger, the little man, and I pass through the tall grasses, heading away from the hillside where I met the plant helper. I haven't yet walked in this direction and am quick to notice the changing landscape. How many different vistas exist here, I marvel to myself. If you don't like one, all you need to do is keep walking, and sooner or later you're bound to find something pleasing. I guess that's true of life itself. If I don't like a situation I am in, I can get up and start moving; at some point I will settle on something delightful, especially if my soul is in the lead. I make a mental note for later reflection: Surrender to yourself.

We continue walking in silence. Occasionally, the tiger jumps up at me, joyfully exhibiting his love for play. With each leap, I feel a smile in my heart and my breathing deepens, drawing in the fresh scents of the land.

Ahead of us I see a stone castle that has to be straight out of a fairy tale. It is surrounded by a perfectly manicured lawn. Swans are bathing in a pond out front. Although this place has been touched by humans, it exudes the energy of harmony.

The trees here are tall and teeming with songbirds that herald our approach. There are peach trees, apple trees, plum trees, and cherry trees—hundreds of boughs laden with my favorite fruits. "Of course," I can almost hear the tree man saying, "you're starting to get the picture."

Actually, the tree man stops beneath an apple tree and says, "Why don't you go inside and explore the castle a bit." As if reading my mind, he adds, "There is no danger here. I think you will find the castle fascinating. We will wait under this tree for you." The tiger nods in agreement and, overheated, drops onto the cool ground.

I leave my friends and approach the huge wooden doors of the castle. I love buildings made of stone and have long fantasized about living in a stone building deep in the woods. I suppose this hermit fantasy is rooted in my old ambivalence about wanting to live, I say to myself. I used to think of a hideout in the woods as comforting, but now I know it signified my avoidance of life.

Entering the great stone building, I am met by a blast of cool air. I expect it to smell moldy, for the castle looks quite old. But the air is fresh, and the entryway surprisingly clean. On its walls are portraits of historical figures—a strange sight after all my recent encounters with unusual life forms. The humans in these paintings appear stiff, serious, and self-important. They seem intent on displaying their authority, not their passion.

Large white wooden doors at the end of the hallway open into a room with high ceilings, long tables, and walls lined with books. It reminds me of an immense library. This room does smell musty; the books, I figure, have been here more years than I can guess.

I step inside, aware of the sounds of my footsteps on the wooden floor. A man seated at one of the tables looks up. He is the first human being I have seen in these worlds.

I approach him slowly, for I don't know if I am welcome. He is quite handsome—with dark brown hair, eyes to match, and features, although not perfect, well-suited to his face. I estimate him to be just under six feet tall. And even though we have never met, there is something vaguely familiar about him. I can't put my finger on what it is, but I can tell that I am strangely attracted to his energy.

I decide to be bold and introduce myself. "I am C Alexandra."

"It's a pleasure to meet you," he replies. "My name is Étienne."

"That name sounds French."

"My mother was French."

"Oh," I say, a little unsure of myself. "What are you reading?"

"I'm reading a book about the teachings of J. Krishnamurti. I think he was a brilliant man. I read as much of his work as I can."

"What does he teach?"

"He explains how to observe and not judge our thoughts and feelings as they arise. He was an empty being, a true spiritual master. He knew how to be of this life yet not attached to it. You should read one of his books."

How appropriate for me, I think to myself.

"Are you from here?" I inquire aloud.

"No. I am here to learn about Krishnamurti and his practice of inquiry. I am trying to improve my life."

"I guess that is why I am here, too. Not to learn about Krishnamurti, but to learn how to live my life in accordance with the laws of nature."

My heart beats rapidly as I speak to this fascinating man. I feel intimidated by him. The cadence of his voice leads me to believe he is highly educated and aristocratic, whereas I am a simple person. I feel crude and clumsy as I stand before him.

He smiles, which relieves me enormously. "Would you like to go outside and sit by the pond? I know a tree that has the sweetest apples."

"Yes, I would love to," I reply.

Étienne gets up. He does stand about six feet, I note. And next to him I feel small—in many ways.

We stroll out of the library, down the long dark hall, and through the huge wooden doors. The tree man and the tiger are nowhere to be seen. Continuing on around the castle, Étienne and I come to a pond with a small waterfall. We sit on the manicured lawn under a tree laden with reddish green apples. The sound of wind chimes and running water add to the peaceful ambience.

I sense that this is Étienne's special place. I feel privileged that he has taken me here.

Étienne asks, "Are you familiar with the practice of meditation?"

"Not really. I have taken some relaxation classes, but haven't formally practiced meditation. What is it like?"

I get the feeling that Étienne is not prone to chitchat. He seems to bypass the typical getting-acquainted questions. Although he is physically handsome, I am more attracted to him on an energetic level. Something about his energy fascinates me. He seems so still inside, free of chaos and confusion. Perhaps he has found the center my helpers in these worlds have been speaking of, I tell myself.

"The art of meditation," he explains, "entails emptying the mind of thought for the purpose of finding your true self. The conditioned mind is governed by thoughts and illusions, but meditation takes you to the truth."

"I could use something like that. I have been learning more about my true self and would like to know how to anchor the experience. Is meditation hard to do?"

"What is difficult about meditation is emptying the mind of the endless chatter it engages in. The mind feels threatened when you try to go beyond it. Sometimes mine will strike out by sabotaging my work.

"One good approach is simply to observe the thoughts and feelings that come up. Just notice them—don't attach to them. I find it helpful to repeat a question such as 'Who am I?' or a mantra such as 'God is love.'"

"Have you been meditating a long time?"

"Since I was a young boy."

"I see. Would you teach me how to meditate?"

"I'll try. It will take a great deal of concentration and focus at first, so we could start by doing it for a few minutes. Then you can work your way up."

I want to get to know this man, I decide, and experiencing his path firsthand seems like a good way to start. I hope we will someday communicate on a more personal level.

"How do we begin?" I ask.

"Just sit in a comfortable position, close your eyes, and breathe deeply. Breath is life, and as you breathe deeply, your energy will begin to rise through your spine, initiating the process. You could start by silently repeating 'Who am I?' as you inhale and exhale."

I shift to a cross-legged position like that of Eastern spiritual teachers in pictures I've seen. I then close my eyes and breathe into my belly, repeating the question "Who am I?"

As I do this, I begin to notice the same expanded feeling I sensed with the tree man. I can't determine where my body begins or ends. My mind is not quiet, to say the least, but I'm not attached to the words floating through it. I simply watch them as though they were clouds drifting across the sky.

I feel my light growing. Yet there is a quality to it I haven't experienced before—something feminine. What I feel, I realize, is my womanness rising within me. I stay with this sensation, enjoying the feeling of being simultaneously expanded and filled with feminine energy.

Suddenly I hear a little cough and my eyes snap open.

"I'm sorry. I didn't mean to disturb you," Étienne says. "While meditating, you also have to observe outside sounds."

"That's okay. I think I've had enough for now."

"Do you want to share your experience with me?"

I tell Étienne about the light and my sense of the feminine presiding in me.

"If you keep up the practice, you will go even beyond that."

"Do you meditate every day?"

"Yes, this is my path."

"What else do you do in your life?"

"I take walks in nature. I play music. My life is really one of contemplation. What about you? What do you do?"

"Up to this point I have been working hard in an office. But I realize now that my life has had no meaning. I must bring in a more spiritual component."

"Do you know what that would entail?"

"I know I would like to spend more time in nature and develop a path of contemplation. I know I want to nurture my body and my soul, and draw more out of my life experience. Figuring out how to do this is a bit over-whelming for me. I am taking in so much information right now that I will need time to adjust to it all. The advice I keep getting is to take things step-by-step."

"That's good advice. I have been lucky—my path has been clear to me. My life has not always been easy, but I have known where I've wanted to focus my attention."

I know that what Étienne says about himself is true, but I sense that something is missing. There's a dry-desert feeling inside me, as if his path does not provide the richness of the earth we are sitting on. There's a stillness in this man's eyes, but not a joy. I begin to wonder what he is thinking about me.

"Have an apple," he offers, reaching up and plucking some fruit off the tree. He hands me a large reddish green apple. I take a bite, savoring its sweetness and juici-ness. Aware that the apple is giving me a gift, I eat slowly, welcoming the life force this tree has shared with me.

I tell Étienne about my experience with the plant helper. He listens intently, his eyes growing wide as I describe how the plants volunteer their spirit and life force to help us. A twinkle begins to replace the stark stillness in his eyes. His face starts to soften.

As I watch Étienne's changing features, I gain new understanding. He has been on a spiritual path with meaning for him, but I long for a path rich with the play and magic I feel with the tiger and the tree man. I loved meeting Jonathan and Leah in the ethereal worlds. I adored meeting the teacher dressed in mid-night blue as I left my hospital bed. But I love the earthiness of this place even more and am drawn most strongly to the richness of life and humor that exists here. How, I wonder, do I bring all these worlds together? Can I share with Étienne the quality of life I have found in these realms? Do I have *anything* to share with this man?

I have a knowing that Étienne has come into my life for a reason. What it is I do not know, though I feel attached to him in an unusual way.

As I recount my adventures, I exude charm. Without intending to, I seem to be courting this man with my energy and words.

Étienne laughs at the antics of the tree man and the tiger. Then he tells me of his travels and his meetings with great spiritual masters. Wit and charm permeate his words as well.

The more stories we share, the more the stiffness between us is released. Soon we are taking in the aroma of the sweet apples hanging from the tree beside us. And we are listening to the breeze as it blows gently through the wind chimes, blending with the delicate rush of the waterfall.

We laugh at the plight of the human mind and swap stories until darkness descends on us. When I realize how late it is, I feel compelled to make contact with the tree man and the tiger.

"I need to find my friends and let them know where I am," I tell Étienne. "Will you wait here for me?"

"Sure," he replies, staring up at the night sky.

"I'll be right back."

I try to get up with grace—an endeavor that proves only semisuccessful. Moving quickly, yet without running, I start to search for my friends, who'd agreed to meet me outside the castle doors. Unable to find them anywhere, I console myself, whispering, "It's okay. I feel fine where I am. I know they will find me when they want to."

I return to the apple tree, only to discover that Étienne has disappeared. Well, maybe he thought I'd be gone longer, I say to myself. I'll just sit here and wait.

I scoot down and rest my back against the tree, searching for a comfortable position. Feeling too fidgety to sit, I lie on the ground and reflect on my extreme vulnerability. I seem attached to starting some kind of relationship with Étienne. The thought terrifies me, for relationships have not been my forte. Most of my romances have been brief. I end up either breaking the man's heart or having mine broken. And each time I decide to avoid a relationship, there I am popping into a new one. I'm searching for something, I conclude.

I keep thinking relationships should be simpler, because we are all seeking love. It makes no sense that personality clashes, jealous feelings, insecurities, and different space needs should always get in the way. Why, I wonder, is it so difficult to find someone I can just love?

I think back to a psychic I once saw, who ended his talk by answering questions from the audience. Troubled by a relationship I was in, I decided to ask if the other worlds would share wisdom with me. I was skeptical of unscientific phenomena, yet so desperate for answers that I was willing to open to supernatural realms. When I asked my question, the psychic closed his eyes and said the name of the man in question. This impressed me, for I had not given him the man's name. I uncrossed my legs and shifted to a more open position.

He went on to inquire, "You are asking me about happiness ever after, aren't you?"

"Yes, I guess I am," I replied.

"There is no such thing as happiness ever after."

My energy fell deep into the earth. What was I supposed to do with this information?

That episode was the beginning of the end for me. I set out to disprove the myth of "happiness ever after," but I could not manage to remove myself from the relationship loop and the consequences of a repeatedly broken heart.

I stare into the night sky. I really want to be with Étienne. Although I don't know him, I feel a longing in my heart for him. A question from the tree man comes floating into my mind: What qualities of yourself are you projecting onto this man?

Maybe I am projecting onto Étienne, I confess. I love his charm and wit and self-assurance. Surely these could be qualities I'd like to see in myself. But projection or not, my female hormones are starting to kick in. I am attracted to this man on levels beyond personality and spiritual knowledge. I want Étienne. And he is not here. What if I never see him again? I guess the hormone stage will pass and I will get on with my life, I reason. I know this scenario pretty well.

I shift my gaze from the beauty of the stars to the sliver of moon just beginning to form. Once again I hear the moon calling to me. I wish I knew how to open to her, I tell myself.

With that, my eyes close, taking me into a deep sleep.

I WAKE UP IN A BED IN THE HOSPITAL ROOM. I AM HOOKED up to monitors of all sorts. What should have been a simple operation has been jeopardized by the great force of nature causing the land to shift. I am in pain and my vision is blurry. I am cold but cannot find the voice needed to ask for help. I can't seem to move my limbs either, perhaps because I am not yet fully in my body.

The door is open, and as I watch the bustle of activity in the hall, my vision begins to clear. I am helpless in this state, I realize. I hope someone comes to check on me soon.

All of a sudden my heart starts to pound. I see Étienne in the hallway talking to some of the nurses. He is holding a bouquet of flowers.

My body is too racked with pain to contain my awareness any longer. I slip back into unconsciousness.

I drift up past stars and planets. I soar through cloud layers and beyond the crystal city where I met Jonathan and Leah and saw the lights about to be born into the world.

At last I arrive at unfamiliar territory in the night sky. From here I can see the moon as she begins her new cycle. I hear water flowing and, looking around, discover that I am by a river. A woman is seated on the riverbank. Moving closer, I see that she is brushing her hair. The sweet fragrance of amber fills the air.

"You can approach," she says in a voice almost too strong for her size.

She stands as I walk toward her, seduced by the power of her presence. She has shoulder length black hair, dark skin, and eyes as black as the night. She is dressed in a cobalt-blue tunic and is adorned with gold jewelry. Her beauty, unlike that of my first teacher, is earthy in a way I can only describe as magical.

"Welcome to my home. I am the goddess Isis," she announces.

"Thank you," I reply. "My name is C Alexandra."

"I know," she says calmly. "I have been watching you for some time."

Her body is firm and robust, exuding love through every pore. She appears unshakable, graced with the energy of unconditional love and immeasurable strength. She is pure feminine power.

Isis returns to her spot by the river and I sit beside her. "I've been watching you with this man you have met," she continues, once again brushing her silky black hair. "What are you calling to you?"

"I want this man," I answer, reminded of the anaconda's warning.

"Do you have any idea what you are asking for?"

"No, but my body is surging with desire and I am willing to take the risk."

"I understand." She stops brushing her hair and looks at me, adding, "Are you calling him to you or are you trusting that he will come to you on his own?"

"I want this man," I repeat.

"Don't use unnatural powers to get him," she implores, "or you will regret it for the rest of your life. If you are meant to be with him, C Alexandra, let him come to you out of his own free will."

"How do I control my female desire? Isn't wanting someone part of courting?"

"Yes and no. It depends on what you are after. If you are seeking a one-night stand, the desire you feel is appropriate. If you are seeking something deeper, you must go beyond this. In my estimation, it seems you want something deeper.

"An untapped feminine power is starting to rise in you. You want that power met. If this is the man to do it, let him walk into your life on his own two feet. If you continue to use the charm you speak of, the magic will eventually wear off. And then where will you be? In another empty relationship leaving in its wake two people stunned by the illusion they have engaged in. Maybe it's time to try something different.

"You are beginning one of the most important

adventures of your life. The lessons you will learn from being in relationship can spark the understanding you seek. True love, remember, replaces all prior knowledge. And you are about to embark on the path of true love."

"But I don't want true love."

"It's too late, my dear," she says with compassion in her eyes. "You have already asked for it."

A PINK-ORANGE GLOW IN THE DAWN SKY WAKES ME UP. My heart is heavy, for it is morning and Étienne has not returned. Moreover, my meeting with Isis has left me feeling afraid and more vulnerable than before. What, I wonder, have I called into my life? What roller-coaster ride have I opted for this time?

I must clear my head, I decide, looking at the pond. It's going to be cold, but a good blast of chilly water is just what I need. Seeing no one about, I remove my purple fleece jacket, slip out of my clothes, and jump into the pond. The water does wake me up. Better yet, it eases all the old fears roused by my desire to be with a man.

The water feels good against my body. As I swim, I imagine merging my cells with the molecules of water, and soon I am feeling myself *as* the water. Water doesn't worry about speed or obstacles, I remind myself; it simply flows from its source, changing its direction and shape as it moves along.

A deep voice pulls me from my oneness with the water. "Good morning."

Startled, I look up. Étienne is standing by the edge of the pond.

"How's the water?" he asks.

"Delicious," I reply. "It's cold, but refreshing. Do you want to join me?"

Étienne takes off his clothes, revealing his muscular body, and jumps in. He's graceful in the water and clearly an experienced swimmer, I observe. He, too, has probably merged with the water spirit—I can tell by the ease with which he dives underwater, surfaces, and plays with the waves he's created. Finally he swims toward me.

Having treaded water all this time, I am a little out of breath.

"I'm sorry I disappeared last night. I hope you didn't take it personally. Sometimes an energy grabs me, and if I don't go with it, I miss an opportunity."

"What do you mean?" I sputter.

"The energy of a spiritual teacher I have been wanting to meet was moving through the field after you left. I needed to follow the pull to meet her, for I didn't know when she would be coming back through."

"I haven't had that particular experience, though I have followed my share of pulls. I must admit I was somewhat taken aback when I realized you weren't returning. I am not the most secure person, and I thought I may have offended you in some way. In any case, it was lovely sleeping out here last night and I had a powerful dream. So I guess it was all perfect."

"Your lips are turning blue. Let's get out of the water."

We kick off together. I have to work hard to keep up with Étienne. Even so, I am comfortable swimming beside him. Being naturally buoyant in water, I feel as though someone is rocking me in a cradle.

When we reach the edge of the pond, Étienne pulls himself out. Turning to me, he says, "I know where to find some towels. Wait here for me. I will be right back and we can dry off."

He disappears through a side door to the castle. He seems familiar with this place, I think to myself, as if he has settled in here. Yet to me the castle and the land surrounding it are imbued with impermanence, as if at any moment they might evaporate into thin air. At times I feel as though my energy is what's keeping them here.

I climb out onto the grass, shake off the excess water, and slip into my fleece jacket. I am sitting huddled beneath the tree when Étienne returns with his arms filled.

"Here you go," he says, gently throwing a long navy-blue towel at me.

"Thanks." I catch it and wrap it around me before pulling off my jacket. I am glad to find that the towel covers me from the neck down, because I'm not quite ready to bare my body to this man, although I would certainly like to.

"You look good in blue."

"Thanks." I'm nervous and short on words.

"Here's a blanket we can sit on." Étienne spreads a red-and-white checkered blanket on the ground.

I lie back on the blanket and watch the rising orange sun. Suddenly I realize how hungry I am.

Étienne, who seems more peppy than yesterday, says, "You must be hungry. Stay here and I will pick some fruit for us."

"Can I help?"

"Just relax. I'm glad to do it."

The sun is starting to radiate warmth. I let its rays nourish my cells. Despite the yearning I feel for the natural rawness of other lands I have visited, I like this place. And I am content to be here with Étienne. Taking notice of his physique has far from squelched my burning desire for him.

He returns with an armful of fruit, which he deposits on the blanket. I sit up, pulling the towel tightly about me. The more snugly wrapped I am, it seems, the calmer I feel.

"Do you want to tell me your dream?" Étienne asks, sitting down and reaching for an apple.

"I'm not sure I am ready to. I met a beautiful teacher with a powerful message, and I need to sit with it a bit." How, I ask myself, can I tell him that it was the Egyptian goddess Isis and that she said I was going to meet my true love?

After a moment I add, "I hope you are not offended by my unwillingness to share. It's just that my experience was so personal."

"Please, I wouldn't dream of invading your space. I'm sure that when you are ready you will share your experience with me."

I like this about Étienne. Whereas I am constantly fighting for space in relationships, he seems to have his boundaries intact. I haven't experienced this trait in other men.

"What about you?" I ask. "Do you want to say who you went off with last night?"

"There's not much I can say, because my experience was quite personal as well. I met up with the Hindu goddess Kali. She has much to relate about death of the ego. It's all part of my practice, you know."

"I, too, met up with a goddess. I visited the Egyptian goddess Isis. Are you familiar with her?"

"I have heard her name, though I have not been drawn to the wisdom of ancient Egypt. What does she have to teach?"

"Well, I'm not sure, because I have just met her. She is an exquisite woman, fully in her power. And she is wise in the ways of the feminine. I look forward to meeting her again."

"That's good. Sometimes these teachers come through for such a brief interval. I hope you will have as much time with her as you want. She must have appeared to teach you something about your own beauty. You are quite beautiful."

Now, I wonder, whose energy is pulling on whose? Has Étienne been calling me to him or have I been calling him to me? How do I sort this one out?

Étienne sets down the apple he has been eating, reaches out and, gently holding my chin, kisses my lips. My mind wants to resist but my body gives in fully, and I meet his lips with the passion I am feeling inside.

We fall to the ground. I lose my towel to the earth as our hands start exploring each other. I am surprised by the depth of passion I feel for him. Although I hardly know him, I find that on some level I know him well: Our chemistry is right and our bodies fit together perfectly. I meet Étienne's male energy fully and wrap around him the fire of my feminine.

We end our lovemaking with a flurry of kisses. Then we lie back on the blanket.

"Wow! I have been fantasizing about you, but I didn't expect *this,*" I comment.

"I felt a connection the moment I met you," he replies.

"I feel one, too. What do you think it is about?"

"I don't know."

"Would you like to explore this?" I inquire.

"Sure, what do you have in mind?"

"When you meditate, you try to get to an empty state. But can you receive intuitions in this state?"

"I can when I need to, and when I am clear enough."

"I learned from the tree man how to relax enough to travel for information. What if you meditate and get

information on our connection while I gather information in the way I have learned? What do you think about
that?"

"I'm game," he says.

Étienne sits up to meditate on the meaning of our
connection. I remain on my back, imagining the tree
man as he instructs me in ways to access help from
beings. Relaxing, I float out of the universe as I know it,
traveling swiftly back through time. I am from another
galaxy looking down onto the earth as it first takes
shape. I decide to explore the earth experience, and at
that moment my soul splits into two energy forms—one
holding the potential of the feminine, and the other the
masculine.

An intelligence begins to speak in a loud, impersonal
tone of voice: "You and Étienne originally entered into
your earth dance as one soul. Étienne is the masculine
part of you, and you are the feminine part of him. You
have been apart for eons, and now you are reuniting to
accompany each other back home."

Jumping into the universe as this energy form, I feel
an excitement flowing through me. I am embarking on
a new adventure. Then instantly, the vision disappears.
My energy collapses back into my body. I open my eyes
and see that I am once again on the red-and-white
checkered blanket by the pond in the sun. My head is
throbbing from the rapid return, and I am not yet
grounded.

I look over at Étienne. His eyes are still closed; his
face appears soft and peaceful; his breathing is quiet. I
love looking at him. Then I lower my eyelids, breathe
deeply, and take an inventory of my body from the feet
up. I sense numbness everywhere. Continuing to breathe
deeply, I feel my body resting upon the blanket on the
earth. I wiggle my toes and little by little bring my atten-

tion upward to my head. At this point the female part of me that wants to be met begins to burn with desire for Étienne. I am back.

Opening my eyes, I see that Étienne is looking toward the pond. Although he and I have just had the most intimate experience two people can undergo, I am not sure I know him well enough to share this vision with. I'll see if he wants to speak first, I tell myself.

With that, I begin talking excitedly. "I had the most amazing vision. You might think it too bizarre, but I have to tell you what I saw." I proceed to relate the entire sequence of events I experienced in my altered state of consciousness. I tell him about leaving the universe and traveling back to the beginning of time, when the earth was born, and about the words spoken by the intelligence.

Étienne listens, all the while gazing at me with his large brown eyes. I can tell that the intimacy of our lovemaking has softened both his gaze and his energy. Without waiting for his response, I ask, "What did *you* get?"

"I saw the same thing."

We look at each other in amazement and burst out laughing.

ÉTIENNE STANDS, WRAPS HIMSELF IN A GREEN TOWEL, AND reaches out a hand to help me up. "Come with me," he says.

I get up, fold the blue towel snugly around me, and follow him to the pond.

There he takes me into his arms and kisses me. Then he sits, gently pulling me down in front of him. "Let's look at our reflections in the water."

I lean back into his inviting body, feeling his warm skin against mine and soaking in the joy of his embrace. Then we scoot forward to peer into the still water.

"We look like brother and sister," I observe.

"Do you think so?" he asks.

"Sure, look closer."

"You're right. In fact, you look more like my sister than my own sister does."

Hearing that he has a sister, I realize how little I know about this man. All the same I feel a deep closeness.

Gazing into the water, I see the reflection of clouds gathering rapidly overhead. The wind picks up and a chill rises in the air. Turning to face the sky, we see enormous black clouds. Suddenly the wind shifts and thunder roars in the distance. Then lightning streaks across the horizon. Just as I'm contemplating how magical it is to watch a storm forming in the sky, a great boom reverberates above us. The clouds immediately open to share their water with the earth.

Part of me wants to stay in Étienne's arms watching the storm, but by now the rain is pouring down in torrents. We dash to the tree to grab our clothes and blanket, then I follow him to yet another door of the castle.

We burst into a carpeted room with our wet clothes, blanket, and towels dragging behind us. The carpet is fluffy and light beige, and set about the room are a huge, stuffed, old-fashioned-looking green couch and several armchairs as well as a cluster of wooden chairs. I shake out my clothes and put them on; Étienne does the same with his. Then we drape our towels and blanket over the wooden chairs.

"Have a seat," Étienne says, as if welcoming me to his home. "I will light a fire for us."

"You seem to know this place quite well. Do you

spend a lot of time here?" I ask him, settling into the couch.

"Actually I do, C. After we dry off, I will take you on a short tour of the castle. I think you will find it interesting."

Étienne builds a cozy fire and sits beside me. There's so much to say, and yet no words pass between us. What, I wonder, do you say to the other half of your soul? Where do we go from here?

"That was an intense message we received," I articulate at last, sinking further into the couch. I haven't known the comfort of soft furniture since my departure from the hospital. And although my body likes the feel of it, something in me rebels against being out of nature and in a manufactured setting.

Étienne stares into the fire. Again he has that empty look in his eyes. "When I check in with myself, the message rings true," he replies. "I just don't know what to do with it. My life, although simple, is very full, and I have so much to explore right now. I need time. Here, come with me and let me show you something."

Almost jumping off the couch, he bounds over to a standing mirror in a corner of the room. I notice an unsettled feeling in my stomach—a sensation I often experience when I think the bottom is about to drop out of my life. Reluctantly I get up and stand beside him.

"This mirror is an entryway to another world," he explains. "Each room in the castle is furnished with one, and with articles from a different place and time period. If I look into this mirror with the intention of entering the time period represented by the room we are in, its surface will at first liquefy and then turn into a gaseous fog that I can walk through. I have spent much time entering a variety of lands and epochs through the mirrors in these rooms. I am not ready to end my explorations, for there is so much more to learn."

"I could come with you on some of your journeys, and you could accompany me on some of mine. We would have great fun traveling together in this way."

"It's not that simple, C. I am a loner who needs a lot of space. I'm not sure I want to share these experiences with anyone at this point. Maybe later, but not now."

"I'm willing to give you the time and space you need. But my intuition says there is more to your reluctance. Are you telling me everything?"

"We can talk about this later. Would you like to explore the castle with me?"

"No, my heart is burning. Let's talk."

"Okay, there is someone else in my life. I didn't plan on what happened between us. The pull was so strong that I didn't think about the future and what we were getting into. Did you?"

"There's someone else in your life?" I am taken aback. "Look, Étienne, it's not that you did anything wrong by making love with me. I wanted it as badly as you. But after what we just experienced together, I can't just say, 'See you—have a good life.' Étienne, I want more. I'm willing to give you time and space, but I will not let you go!"

"C, you have to. I'm not ready for you. I'm not ready for us!"

"How can you do this to me?"

"I'm not doing anything to you. Look, I'm sorry. I didn't mean for you to get hurt. I don't think this conversation can go anywhere unless you settle down and communicate and not blame me for hurting you."

"Well, excuse me if I seem a little upset. I'm just not ready to let such a powerful opportunity for growth dissolve right in front of my eyes."

"I understand, and I am sorry. But I'm not going to participate in hysterical discussions that hurl blame and accusations around the room. I have come too far to resort to this. Let's just sit by the fire and try to center a bit."

I don't know if I can engage in a civil conversation with Étienne. My womanhood feels threatened. My body is on fire and he's telling me he can't meet this fire. I can't speak rationally right now, I tell myself.

"Come, sit with me on the couch. If you want to leave, you can. But if you want to be with me, then sit down."

I begrudgingly move toward the fire and plunk down in a stuffed chair beside the couch. If he wants his space, I tell myself, then so do I! The feelings racing within me are so out of control I'm not sure I can pull this off gracefully.

"How can you do this?" I burst forth, not intending to.

"Look, C, I do love you. But there is a correct time and place for love and commitment. The time is not right for me."

"Who is this woman? Do you love her? Have you told *her* you are not ready for a commitment?"

"Look, I am not going to get into this with you. You are not open to talking and listening. It's as if you only want to blame and accuse. I am sorry that you feel so hurt. I need to leave now."

Étienne jumps up and darts out of the room. I am riddled with questions. Do I stop him or let him go? Can I live with myself if I let him evaporate from my life? No, I decide, for then I will never be able to forgive myself. I need more time with him.

I run out of the room and down the hallway. Feeling his energy to the right, I turn right and come upon an open door. Entering the room, I catch a last glimpse of Étienne moving through the mirror.

I look around the room. The decor is Chinese. To my left is a long table edged with jade carvings; on the wall behind it are panels adorned with red serpents and one-legged dragons; and lining the fireplace to my right are decorative bronze ritual vases. I head for the mirror and ask it to let me enter. The glass turns to liquid, gas, then fog, whereupon I jump through.

I tumble head over heels down a tunnel. I can only assume that my inner turmoil has produced an agitated energy field, which is being mirrored back to me by my passage through the tunnel. I cannot slow down and I certainly can't stop. Finally, I drop to the ground.

This place, like some of the others I have visited, is home to a briskly flowing river. In some spots the current is almost violent. Bordering the river are stands of decid uous trees. I search the woodlands for Étienne, but to no avail. I do not know where I am. All I know is how awful I feel that an experience so beautiful and right could become so ugly. I wish I could have been more gracious, I confess in a whisper. What am I to do with this feeling of loss? It is as though my heart has been ripped out, causing a wrenching pain that will persist for quite some time. I don't want to go through this, I tell myself adamantly.

"Why don't you come sit by me." The voice seems to spring from the river, as if the water itself were speaking—which at this point would not surprise me.

I set off toward the river and soon notice a man hunched over the water from his seat on a rock. Could this be Étienne? I wonder, my stomach momentarily fluttering. I am not aware that desire is blinding me until I discover that the man is quite old. Stepping closer, I see he is Lao-tzu. So we get to meet at last, I declare silently.

"I'm looking for a friend who may have come this way," I say aloud. "Can you help me?"

"I haven't seen anyone pass through here. Why don't you come sit with me by the river."

"I'm feeling a great loss right now, and I do not have the patience to sit and talk. Maybe another time. Now I need to search for my friend."

"I doubt you will find your friend here. Sit down for a moment—the river will help soothe your emotions."

My mind goes into high gear. How could I with any success run around a foreign land looking for Étienne? He could be anywhere. He may even have gone through a different tunnel. Maybe if I sit with this man he will help me.

"You look like a Chinese sage named Lao-tzu, who once lived on the earth," I say, perching on a rock beside him.

"I am the energy you call Lao-tzu."

Although I'm not sure what that means, I go on to tell him, "I saw you in a vision recently. I saw your face, and you looked at me and said, 'You have forgotten everything I taught you.' It was as if you had known me."

"You were once a distinguished student of mine. In the time that has passed since I last saw you, you have forgotten a great deal."

"What have I forgotten?"

"That life is constant change. Watch the river for a moment. It perseveres in its journey back to the source. Twists, turns, and obstacles present themselves, and in response the river continually transforms itself. But it never stops moving.

"Life is like that. Many paths will cross the road you walk along. Many situations will arise to hinder you in your return to the source. You must learn how to move with life. You must learn to bend in response to the natural forces that are moving you, just as the river does, and the stars, the moon, the sun, the wind. Any attempt to halt the natural rhythm of life will lead to a path of disharmony. Stop your white-knuckled navigating and let life take you where it may. There will be rapids as well as smooth waters. Go with the flow."

"I am discovering the importance of flexibility on my own. Is this what I have forgotten?"

"This is a piece of it, and for now an important one to remember."

"When I saw you in my vision, you seemed disappointed in me. Is this true or was it my projection?"

"I honor where your path takes you, C Alexandra. There is no 'right way' to grow. Life is a seed of the light. A tree's branches find many ways to grow toward the sun, the source of light. By the same token, there are many ways for you to grow toward the sun. I honor your path and your journey. I encourage you to be as aware as possible. Don't get lazy. Wake up and live every moment to its fullest."

"Many teachers have told me that life is an adventure I can enjoy. It sounds like you are saying something similar but in different words. You are suggesting that enjoying the adventure has to do with following the natural cycles of life."

"You are correct in this. You are part of nature and must become one with nature's rhythms and nature's clock. You must learn to adhere to the flow."

"I probably already know the answer to this question, but how do I deal with the loss I am feeling? I have just lost a man I am deeply in love with and attached to. I know that in nature cycles of dying precede cycles of rebirth, but right now I feel awful."

"Many little deaths are to be expected in life. You must let the energy of the pain move through you. Don't try to stop it. It's as unnatural to stop pain as it is to hold on to it. Meet the pain, experience it completely, then watch it transform.

"Whenever an energy confronts you from either outside or inside, you must meet it. If you ignore it, the energy will intensify. If you threaten it, the energy will intensify. If you meet it fully, the energy will have no choice but to change. This is the way of nature. So experience your loss fully, and it will have no choice but to change. As the river flows violently over rocks and turns to rapids, it stays true to itself. Because it stays true to itself, the forces of nature return it to a state of tranquillity.

"All the stages you go through in life are parts of your journey. All the states of consciousness you experience are parts of this adventure. Everything changes—that is the one thing you can count on in life. Stay in the moment with your pain and watch the transformation that occurs. Stay awake to the continuing flow of life."

"Thank you for your helpful words. Will I see you again?"

"If the flow of life brings our rivulets back together, we shall meet."

"That is not the response I want to hear. I want to hear, 'Yes, you will see me again. Yes, I will always be with you.' I'm not very comfortable with the unknown."

"The path of life is unknown. This, too, is part of nature. There is no way to stay in the known. There is no way to know what the future will bring. As soon as you think you know what the future holds, you will be presented with an altogether different picture. There is only change, and the changes up ahead are unknown.

"As long as you remember who you are, you will have nothing to worry about. Just stay on the path, taking one step at a time. There is no end; there is only the journey. Try to enjoy the journey."

"I have also received this message before."

"Life is much simpler than you think. The lessons for

you to learn are equally simple. Remember who you are
and that in this life you are part of nature. Receive the gift
of life. Yes, there will be little deaths from time to time,
yet new growth and beauty will replace the blooms that
have died.

"Think of yourself as a growing plant. A plant puts
forth beautiful blooms when it has the energy to do so.
The more it is fed, the less energy it needs for growth. If
at any point your growth requires too much effort, try to
find the needed nourishment. This is your responsibility.
The river of life will take you to many places, but you
must feed yourself along the way. I wish you great joy as
you follow your soul's journey."

"Thank you. I don't know if I will see you again,
though I hope I do. Can you tell me how to get back to
the place I came from?"

"Lie down near the river and rest. While closing your
eyes, hold the intention of getting to where you want to go.
As you drift off to sleep, your dream will take you there."

With these words, Lao-tzu stands up and reaches
behind the rock for his walking stick—a long, curved,
exquisitely carved tree branch. Very soon he disappears
into the woodlands.

The pain of losing Étienne is too fresh for me to even
think about sleep. Besides, I am afraid that if I leave this
place I may never find him. Not meaning to, I become
entranced by the river. Watching the water as it hurdles the
rocks releases some of my fears. The strength of the current pulls the pain out of my heart. I reflect on the many
healing experiences I have had with water in these new
worlds. Since I can't explore my relationship with Étienne,
I resolve, I will explore my relationship with water. It
soothes my soul in ways I have never before experienced.

The roar and spray of the river pull my energy down.
Feeling sleepy at last, I head for a small beach off to my

right and stretch out in the cool sand. The rush of the river drowns out my thoughts and feelings, giving rise to a delicious peace.

My consciousness drifts into a blissful dream state. Having received no directive to return to the castle, my dream carries my soul to a new place—an ethereal land beyond the stars. I am floating among clouds as if drifting in a serene sea. Suddenly I sit up, surprised to find that I am not alone, but rather with a woman formed mostly of light. She is wearing a long, flowing, pastel yellow and blue robe that radiates with the light emitted from her body.

I introduce myself to the robed figure and ask, "Who are you?"

"In your world I am known as Mary."

To sit in the presence of Mary's energy is awe inspiring. Rays of pastel light emanating from this great being bring light to the places shrouded within me, including the darkness in my heart. I see now that I cannot lose my light, much as I may forget about it. This forgetting, I tell myself, is what my first teacher meant when she said there will be many things to distract me in my travels. How, I wonder, could I have been so easily pulled out of myself by one human being?

Mary cuts through my thoughts with a transmission of unconditional love and compassion. Unconditional love, as I know it in ordinary reality, is the sort of love a puppy gives. A puppy will love its owner no matter how he behaves toward it. A puppy doesn't know how to close its heart.

"You seem troubled, my daughter," Mary begins. "Please tell me of your distress."

I am astounded that the ultimate feminine essence of love would regard me as her "daughter." If I am her daughter, why don't I experience her love in my life? And why don't I know how to express the love she advocates giving? Why do I wall off my heart so readily?

"What is troubling you, my daughter?" Mary reiterates.

I am surprised that she doesn't respond to my thoughts. I had hoped she would read my mind and answer my questions like the other beings have.

I answer superficially, "My heart suffers from a loss."

"I feel your pain, and it lies much deeper than the loss you carry. Your heart is burdened with something other than loss. Will you share your burden with me?"

"I'm afraid the loss covers up whatever pain you are detecting, Mary."

"You must forgive yourself."

"Forgiving myself is not something I have mastered."

"But your guilt is killing you, my child."

"I know. I have felt guilty my entire life. But I have never been able to figure out what I have done to prompt such guilt. I feel that I have done something wrong and should be punished."

"You punish yourself with your guilt."

"Let's take my current situation. I met this man, Éti-enne. We shared love. Then I pressured him for more than he was ready to give. My attachment and desire sought to cling to him. When he expressed a need for space, I used stinging words to hurt him. He doesn't deserve that. Once again I have hurt someone because I didn't get what I wanted. And now I am left feeling unfinished and in pain—and guilt-ridden for having wounded a good man with my words."

"Can you feel compassion for yourself?"

"Yes, on some level I can feel compassion for my pain. But mostly I feel overly responsible to others. Mary, please help me with my guilt."

"Guilt about—?" she asks.

"About not loving enough."

"Have you given your love?" she asks.

"Yes, but I have caused injury with it."

"Is there something you feel you owe?"

"Yes," I reply.

"Then it is not true love. True love is given freely. True love carries no debt. Let go of the debt—you owe nothing. Just give your love.

"As Étienne told you, he cannot be responsible for your happiness or your pain. Nor can you be responsible for his happiness or his pain. No one can be God for another person. No one carries this much responsibility."

I can't believe I am about to disagree with Mary, but I do. "I am familiar with the concept that we create our own reality and are responsible for our own lives. Recently I have gotten this message in spades. But what about personal responsibility? Where does responsibility for my behavior come in? I can't just go around hurting people because I feel hurt, and then letting go of all judgment pertaining to my actions."

"There are many levels to this question. It seems you have given it much consideration. Please speak your thoughts out loud to me. I want to hear them."

"When I was younger, I experimented with mind-altering drugs and had spiritual experiences. I would go to this great light whom I named God. I was struck by the pure love this being emanated, which was similar to the love I feel from you. But God did not speak to me. In fact, he had no identity from which to speak, no form—just pure light. I had the experience of being such a light during one of my recent travels. Anyway, I knew when I first met God that this energy would love me whether I performed saintly deeds or injurious ones. I felt no judgment from him.

"One time after taking a mind-altering substance, I met a female and male energy that exhibited the love and light I feel from you. I called them Mother-Father God. For hours they sat on a bench and repeated to me, 'Forgive yourself. We forgive you.'

"But I don't know how to do that. I feel a need to take responsibility for my actions rather than absolve myself of all sin. Do you understand what I am saying?"

"Yes, the role of the mother and father essence is simply to love and not judge while one learns the lessons one was born to learn. You look at the small picture, for that is what you have been shown. The larger picture must be viewed as well.

"Let us focus on your present situation, as it is fresh in your mind. Is it possible that Étienne needed to experience how his actions hurt you? Étienne, you see, began a deep exploration with you, however brief it may have been. Then he disappeared because he needed space. Yes, maybe there was a more skillful way to share your feelings. And yes, you are reaping what you have sown. But so is he. One plants a seed and watches it grow; seeing the sprout that comes up helps determine whether or not a different seed should be planted next time. This is how we learn. The law of the universe is that one must experience what one has planted. In some lands, people speak of 'reaping what you sow'; in others, the word for this is *karma*. The judgment you speak of has nothing to do with this law of the universe. There is no judgment, as you experienced upon meeting the energy you call God.

"By being so hard on yourself you become stuck, leaving no room for evolution. What you must do instead is *learn* from your behavior. This you can do by

reflecting on your actions and deciding to act differently in the future. Feeling guilty about your past does not
allow for change. Worse yet, it leaves no room for compassion to come your way from either yourself or energy
forms like me.

"Love is what you seek. Without love, the plant that
is you cannot be nourished. Without nourishment, it will
not live.

"Your choice is clear. Do you wish to receive the love
of the universe or do you wish to refuse this love and die?
No longer do you have the luxury of indulging in self-
blame and judgment.

"If you want to live your life fully, then start by loving
yourself as we love you—or, to use your metaphor, as a
puppy would love you. Open up to the grace of love!"

With these words, she puts her hand on the crown of
my head. I am flooded with so much love and light that
I lose consciousness.

I GRADUALLY BECOME AWARE THAT I AM FLOATING. I CANNOT
feel my body, or even open my eyes. I am emotionally
numb as well. Only my mind is awake and, for the first
time in a long time, free of chatter.

I hear a series of words uttered in a monotone: "You
must heal the split."

"What split?" I ask.

"You have asked about Étienne. You are one soul.
You must heal the split."

"I can't heal the split. He won't talk to me."

"You must heal the split."

I am exasperated but surprisingly indifferent to this
conversation. "I cannot heal the split."

"Then you will never again experience happiness in your life."

I am still numb, but suspecting that something here will have future significance, I probe further. "What do you mean I will never again experience happiness in my life? That's insane. I don't believe you!"

"You and Étienne are one soul. Your mission in this lifetime is to heal the split. The rupture between all warring parties on your planet is caused by the sense of separation, which leads to this sort of fear and anger. You must heal the split. You must help other people heal the split."

"I can try to heal the split within me, if that's what you mean."

"You do not understand. The time for working with yourself is over. It is now time for you and your people to heal the split by being in relationship with one another. You must heal the split with Étienne or you will not know happiness."

I have no idea who this intelligence is or where he has come from. All I know is that there is no love in his voice and no compassion in his words.

As my awareness continues to drift, I realize that the voice has gone and all that remains is silence. Instantly, my mind becomes flooded with brightly colored geometric shapes. I don't know where I am. I don't know how to get out of here.

A HAND TOUCHING MINE SHATTERS THE NUMBNESS IN MY body. "Who's here?" I call out with my mind.

"It's Isis. I have come to take you from this place. Just be still and keep your eyes closed. I will lead you by the hand."

I keep my eyes closed and float safely in the care of Isis. We begin moving downward. As waves from the descent rush through me, feelings return to my body. I am dizzy and nauseous.

Finally we reach the home of Isis. She lays me on the ground and summons me to open my eyes. It is dusk, and the sky is tinged with a lavender hue that is soothing to my eyes. Still whirling a bit, I close them once more.

"Breathe this," Isis urges, placing a strong scent under my nose.

"What is it?" I ask, inhaling a second time.

"It's the sage plant. Its aroma will help you come back into your body. Just try to relax. Let your breath carry light back to your body. You have been through quite an experience."

I follow her advice. Then I open my eyes, take in the darkening sky, and close them again. This action seems to help me reenter my body. But I am not yet ready to move. So much has happened that I want only to rest here on the cool, moist ground.

Isis begins massaging my feet while humming a gentle, soothing tune. After a while her singing grows louder. Soon her voice fills the air with a range of intervals, sounding like a large choir. Her toning is so grounding that my nausea and dizziness vanish, leaving only exhaustion.

I fall into a deep slumber. This time my consciousness as well as my body gives over to the peace of sleep.

I awake on a soft futon in an open-air room. The morning sun is streaming through a canopy of purples and blues over my head. Focusing more closely, I notice that long pieces of silk tied loosely to wooden posts in the corners of the room are creating this soft, wispy ceiling.

Isis appears at my bed holding a tray made of woven

grasses. On the tray is an assortment of breads and fruit. I am ravenously hungry, as though I haven't eaten in ages.

"How long have I been sleeping?" I ask, eagerly stuffing a piece of bread into my mouth. I am too hungry to concentrate on taking in the "gift" of the grains.

"You have been sleeping for half a cycle of the moon," Isis replies.

"You mean I slept while the moon rose and fell in the sky?"

"No, C, you have been sleeping for half a cycle of the moon."

"But that is two weeks, isn't it?"

"Yes, in your time that would be considered a fortnight."

"How can that be? How could I have slept so long?"

"You had a great deal to integrate. You called in many powers here, and your calls were all answered. The time to rest had come. And what better place was there to do it than by the healing Nile?"

"I don't know anything about the Nile, but thank you for providing me with such a wonderful resting place."

"Finish eating, then come join me on the banks of the river," she says, exiting with an air of grace and ease.

This woman is certainly not burdened with insecurity or guilt, I tell myself, finishing the food a bit more slowly than I began. Although I am reticent to leave this safe, comfortable setting, I rise to meet Isis at the Nile. On a soft chair by my bed I notice a green silk dress. I put it on, surprised to find that it fits perfectly. Feeling the softness of the silk against my body, I realize that I need to be nurtured not only by the food I eat but by the fabrics I wear and the colors I surround myself with.

I leave the room running my fingers through whatever strands of hair are not matted to my head. The knots catching my fingers alert me to the fact that these tangles will not be fun to comb out.

Isis is waiting for me by the river. The only other time I remember being here was in the darkness of night. I look around at the greenery, which I hadn't noticed before. The tall grass reminds me of the tiger, the tree man, and the meadow in which the energy of play reigned supreme. Although aware that time has a different meaning here than in my ordinary life, I begin wondering what has happened to my two friends who were supposed to meet me outside the castle.

"Have a seat," Isis says, greeting me with her smiling dark eyes. "You look beautiful in green. How does it feel to wear it?"

"It feels great."

"Are you aware of the effect of colors on you?"

"I know I am attracted to certain colors at certain times, depending on my mood. My favorite has always been blue. When I need to feel power, I am drawn to that color. But I like green a lot, too."

"Green is a healing color for your body. I'm glad you have been aware of the feelings you get from colors. It will be good to wear those that are the most soothing when you need tranquillity and the most empowering when you require courage.

"I have some wonderful soaps made of healing oils. You are welcome to choose one to use in the water."

I select a soap that smells of lavender and set it beside the river. Then I remove the green dress and, naked, step into the water. It is warm enough to float in, so I allow myself to be buoyed by the gentle waves before washing a fortnight of travel from my skin. As I drift toward the bank, I lower my feet until they are met by the wonderful softness of mud.

Standing, I reach down, squeeze the mud through my

fingers, and pick up handfuls of it to spread over my arms. I cover myself with the soft, wet earth, and then dive underwater to wash it off. Next I scrub myself with the lavender-plant soap and wash that off, too. When I feel squeaky clean all over, I climb onto the grassy riverbank.

Isis, who has been weaving a basket, sets down her creation. The sun is hot, and I am dry almost as soon as I sit beside her.

She arranges several glass containers in front of me. "Pick an oil you would like to have on your skin."

I decide to stay with the lavender fragrance I used for bathing. While I rub the oil into my neck and shoulders, Isis takes several drops of it and begins stroking my feet. In the midst of my elation I notice a sinking feeling pushing its way into my awareness until I am flooded with the disappointment of unrequited love.

As if responding to my inner state, Isis applies pressure to the soles of my feet. "You met an energy that has affected you deeply," she says. "This is good."

"Well, I am not sure what is so good about it. I feel hurt, empty, and raw. I met a formless being who told me that unless I heal the split between Étienne and me, I will never again experience happiness. If he is right, my life is now a mess for even if I were to find Étienne, I would not want to convince him to return to me. I would want him to come back on his own. Come to think of it, I'm not even sure I am ready for a relationship.

"Isis, am I never again going to experience happiness? Who was this intelligence? What an awful message to deliver!"

"The split you are experiencing has ended a period of innocence in your life. The fall from innocence is a powerful initiation. Yes, you will experience happiness again, with or without Étienne. But happiness will have a different meaning, because you are no longer innocent."

I understand her words. I feel like I have awakened from the peaceful, innocent sleep of a child.

"You do not need Étienne in your life. Tell me, what is it about him that you miss?"

"I miss his touch. I miss our lovemaking. I have never felt such ecstasy—emotionally, spiritually, or physically—as I did during our short time together. I miss his charm, his humor, his self-assurance. How's that for a start?"

She laughs. "Your physical attraction to him is quite strong. Yet even if you don't come to know such a power again, at least you will have tasted of its gift; and that experience will always live in your heart. But I am sure you will again feel a power such as this in your life.

"Étienne mirrored qualities you have overlooked in yourself. It's important to own this projection. You see, *you* are charming, humorous, and self-assured. So fill the emptiness you now feel with the qualities you miss in Étienne. Heal from the inside out. All healing occurs in this way."

Isis lowers my feet gently to the grass, stands up, and begins combing out my tangled hair. Feeling the knots come loose, I recall Our Lady of Guadalupe, who also spoke of healing from the inside out. The message I am picking up on is clear: As you change your internal world, your external one will change, too.

"You have had a conversation with the energy called Mary," Isis notes as the sun begins dipping toward the horizon.

"You know where I am all the time, don't you?"

"We are kindred souls. I go where you go."

"I see."

"No, I don't think you do, but let's return to the matter at hand. Your feelings of guilt have been strong—did Mary help you with these?"

"How can I say Mary didn't help me? To my mind, she is the great healer. Being in her presence was extraordinarily healing. Her words held great power and truth. But no, I cannot say I have been healed of my feelings of guilt. I guess that will take time.

"I'd like to embrace what she said about not feeling indebted when I give love, but I have always felt the pain of others. It's hard enough to be around people in pain, and it's that much harder when I am the cause of it. I don't want anyone to have to suffer. I would rather be in pain than watch someone suffer."

"Your boundaries are clear, though, aren't they?" Isis asks. "Do you know the difference between your pain and someone else's?"

"Often I become lost in suffering without knowing its source. But occasionally I can stop myself, aware that I am feeling someone else's feelings."

"Empathy is important in a healer."

"But I am not a healer."

"Conducting formal healings is not the only way to be a healer. Many who do not call themselves healers are healing all the time. When you listen to others with a sympathetic ear, you are healing them. The key is to avoid taking on their pain. Feel it—which you will do, because you are sensitive—then let it pass through you, knowing that in the process a healing has taken place.

"Do you remember your talk with Lao-tzu? He reminded you that one must fully experience an energy for it to pass through and be released. The problem is that you get caught up in the release.

"You cannot save another person; you can only save yourself. You cannot carry the pain of another, no matter how dear that person is to you. But by sitting with others you can empower them while the strength of their own spirit carries them through the void. You received this lesson yourself. It is now time to bring it to your relationships with others."

"How do you help a person who has lost faith in herself?" I ask.

"Have you ever found yourself in such a situation?" Isis inquires.

"Yes, at times in my life I have lost faith in myself and in God."

"Did anyone come in and rescue you?"

"No, no one could have rescued me from this dark place."

"And yet you survived. What happened?"

"I guess when I hit absolute bottom something inside me takes over. Some observer part of myself calmly lets me know that everything will be okay. This observer doesn't get caught up in the suffering or the drama."

"That's the spirit part of you. What you have been learning in your journeys to these worlds is that you have a spirit that cannot be touched by any person or event, including death. The spirit cannot be hurt and cannot die. When the ego part of you shatters, as it does when you lose faith in everything around you, your spirit has a chance to shine through. You recognized this yourself during your trek through the cave, when you sang, 'The strength of my spirit will carry me through the void.'"

"Yes, but I guess now I need to hear about it again."

"That's fine. Don't judge yourself for having to hear a message more than once. Sometimes we need reminders to help us recall what we have forgotten.

"As for helping *others* who have lost faith, remember that the loss of faith is a fall from grace. When you allow spirit to help you regain your faith, what a tremendous initiation that is. What a memorable learning! You become cognizant of a reality larger than everyday life and acquire a stronger foundation to stand on.

"Once you know this is true for you, you'll know it pertains to everyone around you. Being there to listen to another person's pain is the first step in helping him regain faith in himself. The second is to hold the energy for him—to provide a container of love that will allow his spirit to come through.

"The trick for you is to avoid taking on his pain. Actually, it is an illusion to think you can do such a thing; you cannot even know his pain. Hence you end up projecting yours onto him. What you are seeing is your pain in his eyes."

Conversing with Isis has held my attention so completely that I have forgotten my own state of being. I take a quick survey of my feelings. While aware of all I have yet to learn, I do not feel overwhelmed. And although my heart still longs for Étienne, a calmness has replaced the burning inside me. Lao-tzu, I know, would remind me of the impermanence of these circumstances; he would encourage me to ride the ebb and flow of emotions, and avoid attaching myself to one state or another. Here I am sure I can practice this exercise, though I make no pretenses about ever mastering it.

"Our time together is nearing its end," Isis explains gently. "Before you leave, I have one more question to ask you: Why do you count on the beings of nonordinary reality to read your mind? Why don't you just come out and say what you want to say? Why don't you ask for what you want? You seem to place the responsibility on us to know what you need and want, isn't this so?"

"Sometimes when you read my mind, you are seeing through to dynamics I am unaware of—but not this time. It is true that I expect others to know of my needs. I am often disappointed when people do not respond to my silent requests.

"This has been a pattern of mine. I expect others to

know of my pain and my desires. Then I get mad when they don't respond by giving me what I want. I end up getting angry at the insensitivity of others, all the while victimizing myself. The worst part is that I am often conscious of doing this, Isis."

"It is learned behavior that comes from your culture. And always it is self-defeating."

"I know, especially in light of all I have learned recently. I am aware that no one will give me what I want unless I ask for it. I am also aware that even then I will not necessarily get it; but I must at least take the risk and ask for it. This is an important lesson in creating a good life for myself. I must stand in my power and ask for what I want."

"In addition you must be aware of the unconscious desires, beliefs, and attitudes that are governing you. You must learn to distinguish your voice from all the others shaping your creations."

"I know what you mean. My belief that I don't deserve love originates in a voice from the past. So, too, does my certainty about the scarcity of love. I allow these voices to shape my present creations, which are destined for failure because they are fueled by erroneous notions."

"You're learning very well. Your creations are woven by your desires and beliefs. But unless you are aware of the false beliefs and attitudes emanating from voices of the past, you will weave these into your creations as well."

"Isis, there's more I need to ask you, but at the moment a giant magnet seems to be pulling on my solar plexus. What shall I do?"

"We will finish our conversation later. For now, you must follow the pull, because someone else wishes to speak with you."

I look at the sky, and my eyes lock on the waning

moon. Instantly I am yanked away from Isis. Losing sight of the moon, I tumble backward through space. A giant magnet is pulling on me, and I have no choice but to surrender to it.

I LAND ON THE GROUND WITH A THUMP. BEFORE ME IS A woman whose presence could take up worlds. She is sitting cross-legged staring at me. Her eyes are fierce, burning with raw power and angry energy. Avoiding her gaze, I visually stake out my new turf—a stark desert. The ground, a light sand color, holds no vitality. Even the yellowish gray rocks are bare.

Startled by the contrast between this intensely animated woman and her desolate surroundings, I glimpse at her face.

Again she meets my gaze with fierce, catlike eyes. I don't take her anger personally, for it is not directed at me.

"I am the Aztec earth goddess Tonantzin," she says.

"I am C Alexandra," I reply.

"I know—I have called you here. I have a message for you and the people of your time."

I inhale deeply to create more space within me. If I can expand enough to contain her energy, I tell myself, I will not be blown out by her power.

She begins her message. "What you see here is the outcome of people's behavior toward the earth. Man does not have to conquer the earth and her women to get what he wants. He must instead learn to work in partnership with this feminine energy. In addition, he must learn to abide by the feminine energy within himself.

"This is what happens when people think they can

conquer nature," she states, extending her arms, turning at the waist, and pointing at the landscape around us. "Everything dies when man stops honoring the feminine. The earth, as you can see, is unable to withstand the anger and abuse directed toward her. Soil that is not honored cannot sustain plant life; already the vegetation on your planet has little nourishment to offer. Without plant life, the animals go hungry; hence they, too, offer little nourishment for the people. The live foods growing on your earth, like the artificial ones manufactured there, lack soul. Food without soul provides no nourishment. Deprived of the emotional, spiritual, and physical nourishment of plants and animals, humanity loses its soul.

"The soul of your planet is leaving. If the departure proceeds at its current rate, this is what you will see." Again she sweeps her arms through the air, directing my attention to the landscape.

Struck by the bleakness of her vision, I hardly know what to say.

"The earth has had a long life—much longer than humankind can grasp. Relative to this time span, the duration of 'conquest thinking' has been but a flash. The problem, however, is grave, for the energy of conquering leads to more conquering, which ultimately results in the obliteration of all life."

Words finally come to me. "Why are you telling me this? Is there a way out or are we doomed to extinction?"

"There is a way out. The feminine must be encouraged to rise again. The women of your world must tap back into their feminine energy and work together to care for the children. It is time for the women to rise up and say, 'We will not stand by and watch children starve to death.' What kind of mother stands passively by while her children are being killed? Only one who has given up her soul.

"The men of your world must connect with the feminine within them and declare, 'We shall no longer strive to conquer nature or one another. We refuse to participate in destruction.'

"The goddess must be honored. The goddess in each woman, man, and child on your earth must be honored! If this does not happen, the earth will lose her soul. Without soul, there is no essence with which to bestow nourishment. And without nourishment, there is no life. The decision, as always, must be made collectively."

"What am I supposed to do? I am only one person among billions. How can I possibly effect a change of this magnitude?"

"Portions of your soul have been retrieved, have they not?" she asks.

"Yes," I reply.

"Then when you go home and look around you, the people you'll see will not be mirroring back your soulfulness."

"The lack of life force is something I have already seen, Tonantzin. I don't think this will be new to me."

"What will be new, C Alexandra, is that you will no longer be able to dissociate from what you see. You will be forced to make changes in your life and to start awakening the people around you.

"You will do this because the feminine forces—within in you and without—can no longer watch the children starve. These forces have been oppressed for thousands of years. Find the goddess in yourself, then help women and men find her in themselves. You must do this!"

Wondering how to go about such a task, I start thinking out loud. "If I hold this as an intention, will the path be shown to me?"

"The feminine has withstood her oppression and found in the midst of it lessons needed for her evolution. Consequently, help will be available to you from seen and unseen forces, and yes, your path will be revealed to you. That does not mean, however, that it will be free of obstacles. Help restore honor, beauty, and balance, C Alexandra. The goddess will be most grateful."

"I have met a guardian spirit in these worlds who told me that the view of the earth as diseased and imperfect is just an illusion, that really the earth cannot be hurt by human beings. I am trying to reconcile his message with yours."

"What your guardian spirit has shared is true when seen from a higher dimension. From the dimension in which you live, conquering behavior causes scarcity, disease, and in the end, death. If people in your dimension want a life full of soul and abundant resources, then they must learn to live in partnership with all of life.

"The only thing to be destroyed is the god they call gold. Humankind has sold its soul to gold, only to find that it cannot buy happiness, bliss, or nourishment. The death and destruction wrought by the worship of gold is unconscionable. Maintaining one's soul and the well-being of children is far more important than amassing gold.

"Feeding the children is quite simple. First, you must honor the rain gods, the life in plants and animals, and the food sources plucked from the soil. Next, you must relearn how to work with the cycles of nature and the forces of the moon. Finally, you must rediscover that to grow, life forms require love.

"The cause of the present dilemma is the wounding of the male. I have deep compassion for this woundedness, but it is time for the male and the female in every person to shake hands and say, 'I am sorry. Let's get on with life.'"

"This information inspires me. I can see that in addition to remembering my light I have a mission to attend to."

"All people need a mission—for without one, their attention is drawn to the meaninglessness of their existence, perpetuating the conquering mentality. They begin to yearn for power over another to help them feel powerful and meaningful. Thus far, this dynamic has not worked for anyone.

"You live in a very dark time. Much needs to be accomplished. You will find that every individual on your earth has a particular life path as well as a unique talent. The bliss that is sought cannot be purchased; it must be earned by following one's life path. Those who are asleep will need to wake up from the many illusions enveloping them and will need to get in touch with their strengths. It is time for each person to stand up and take his or her rightful place on earth. It is time for each person to share that place on earth with all of life. Then the children shall live."

"Tonantzin, I am most grateful—" Before I can finish the sentence she is gone. The moment she disappears, her pull on me is released and I disappear from the bleak desert setting.

Now I am back in the void that is so full of life. I hear a voice. "This is the place of creation. This is the place in which it all begins. State your intention to the Creator."

"I wish to help people retrieve their souls. I wish to help people remember the feminine power of life so that we all may live," I say. "I ask that I may be helped in my work. I ask that the path be shown to me."

HAVING FALLEN ASLEEP IN THE VOID, I AWAKEN TO A SHARP pain in my solar plexus. The pain catapults me back through the veils between worlds until I am in my hospital room. I land beside the bed on which my body rests in a state of limbo. A girl about five years old is standing on the other side of the bed.

I can tell that she is not in her body and that what I am seeing is her soul. "Who are you?" I ask.

"Lisa," she replies, with a look of terror in her blue eyes.

"What are you doing in this room? Are you lost?"

"I am looking for a home."

I start to get the picture. I remember hearing an unbelievable story from a friend who had been hospitalized for an operation. One night he awoke to a man trying to step into his body. He had to literally fight for occupancy. He later learned that other people had experienced lost souls trying to steal their bodies. Convinced that my friend was hallucinating, I had never given his account a second thought . . . until now.

"Lisa, do you know where your body is?" I ask the child.

"They took it away," she answers, looking down. "I don't know where to go. I am so lonely."

My heart leaps out to Lisa. Because I haven't a clue how to assist her, I call out with my mind, "Can anyone help me?"

Within a moment, Isis appears at my side. Placing her hand on my shoulder, she says, "Lisa's body has died, but her soul has not made the transition out of this world. Her soul is stuck here. We can help her move on."

With that, Isis gracefully approaches the other side of the bed, where Lisa's little soul is standing in despair. Moved to tears by this touching scene, I watch Isis kneel down, look into the child's eyes, and stroke her curly blond hair. The terror in Lisa's big blue eyes seems to vanish.

"Lisa, my name is Isis, and I am here to help you. Would you like me to take you to a better place?"

"Yes."

"Do you remember your grandmother?"

"Yes, she was always nice to me. She gave me candy whenever I wanted it. She died, you know."

"Yes, I know," replies Isis. "Would you like to see your grandmother again? She's waiting to give you a big hug and kiss."

Lisa pauses a moment, trying to make sense of what Isis is suggesting. She is evidently too young to understand that she is dead and that her soul is stuck in this world.

"How can you take me to her?" she finally asks.

"Let's call her," says Isis.

Lisa calls, "Grandma, Grandma, please help me!"

A tunnel of light forms diagonally across the room. Within the tunnel appears the image of an elderly woman. She has short gray hair and a face soft with wrinkles. She exudes great love.

"Lisa," she says. "Come to me. I will take you to your beautiful new home."

Lisa runs into the arms of her grandmother. As Isis promised, the child is greeted with a big hug and kiss. Together they float into the tunnel, taking the light with them.

I turn my attention to my body lying unprotected and vulnerable on the bed. I'd better not remain disconnected from my body much longer, I caution myself. I must return from my soul travels soon.

"Isis, is there a way to protect my body until I am ready to return?" I ask.

She lifts her arms and, running her hands over my body, surrounds me with a translucent blue light. "You will be protected for now," she says.

Isis and I then step into the corridor. All is quiet here, leading me to believe that it must be late at night. A few nurses are gathered at the nurse's station, but they seem too tired to talk. I worry about them working in this state of exhaustion. A light of compassion flows from their hearts, but it is partially concealed by the fatigue of their bodies. Our lives are so out of balance, I think to myself sadly.

I glance at the clock on the wall. It's 4:00 A.M. and dead silent. All I can think about is how sterile everything looks. The walls, the floor, the ceiling, all are barren and colorless. The only smells are those of chemicals and medications.

Isis and I stroll to the window at the end of the hall and perch beneath it on a heater box. I lift the blinds, expecting to see darkness outside, but the streetlights blind me to the night. A light drizzle, combined with the glare of the lights, blocks my view of the sky.

Cars moving along the wet asphalt below produce a hypnotic sound that captures my attention. "I want to come back to my body and to my life here," I say to Isis. "Many of the places I have been visiting are beautiful. Yet here, although modern technology has eased our lives by protecting us from the harshness of nature, we have forgotten the beauty of the world we are a part of."

"It is time for you to invite spirit into your life again," Isis advises. "Many spirits are available to help you. They will help anyone who chooses to reconnect with them. Do you think you can teach people about this?"

"People are afraid of the invisible worlds, Isis. They regard what they cannot see as evil. Indoctrinated into believing only in human authority figures, they fear they will be hurt by spirits. Direct revelation is not supported in my culture. The teaching process will be long and hard."

"Have you been hurt by any of the spirits you have met during your travels?"

"No, I have been met only by love. Even the toughness of the anaconda and of the intelligence who urged me to heal the split was an expression of helpfulness and love."

"Then that is what you must share. Tell people about your encounters. Some will want to experience this sort of love; others will not. Rather than trying to convince anyone, simply open the door to the realms of spirit. Help people get back in touch with their souls. Remind them of their connection to each life form on the planet. You can do this.

"Evil exists only in the mind, in the ego's separation from the web of life. When one feels separate, harmful words and actions ensue. The spirits, however, have never separated from the source, have no egos, and have no need to harm. So you see, one of the great challenges of a human being is to be a creative individual while maintaining contact with the source. This is not an easy task. But yes, it can be done. Disconnectedness from the source and from nature is a fall from grace; the reconnection is a fall to grace.

"For people to experience true happiness, they must learn to reconnect with the source and with nature . . . You like to dance, don't you?"

Entranced by the streetlights and pitter-patter of the rain, I answer indifferently, "Yes, I do. But I haven't danced in quite a while."

"Think back to when you had a good time dancing with a partner."

"I can remember one of those times."

"To create beautiful dance movements with a partner, one must be fully engaged in the dance. Can you imagine what would happen if you were constantly looking around at what others were doing?"

"I wouldn't be able to connect with my partner."

"Exactly. Your dance with the spirits you have met is beautiful, and it will continue. Your earth dance with your own soul and with nature can also be beautiful. What you must learn is to stay engaged with your partners, the rhythms, and the movements. Don't worry about what others are doing. Instead, show them how to find their own dancing partners in the spirit world and in the world of nature."

"This is a powerful metaphor. I will remember it as I continue my soul's journey on earth. Thank you, Isis. Thank you for coming into my life."

Having taken in all I can for now, I lean my head against the cool window and let the soft sounds of the rain lull me into unconsciousness.

WAKING UP IN THE VOID, I SEE A DOOR. WAIT, I SAY TO myself, it's not a door—it's a mirror. I float toward it, excitedly setting my intention to go through it and meet up with the tree man and the tiger, who I assume have returned to the meadow. I yearn to feel the earth beneath me, for it has become my home. I want to go home, I call out silently.

Suddenly the mirror fogs over. Entering the mist, I find myself in a steep tunnel carpeted with rich, dark earth. I climb upward and emerge from the base of a tree on the castle grounds. Glad to be at least in familiar territory, I feel certain of finding my way to the meadow.

Standing on the manicured lawn, I realize with regret that humanity has even conquered the grass. I close my eyes, take a few deep centering breaths, and reflect on my meeting with Tonantzin. Her fierceness inspired me to feel good about returning to my life. Moreover, she gave me a reason to live. I now know what I need to do, only I don't know how to do it—a complication that does not bother me.

The air here is full of life. I receive the offering and, with my eyes still closed, allow it to nourish my cells. I am convinced that my task is to learn how to receive the nourishment around me. And to do this I must, as Mary reminded me, let go of the feeling that I do not deserve love.

Opening my eyes, I see that I am not only on the manicured lawn but near the pond. I skip over to the cool water and splash some on my face. Then I look up and open myself to the warmth of the sun. Realizing how famished I am from the lack of nourishment in the land of Tonantzin, I resolve never to live in a place of such desolation.

"Are you hungry?" The voice comes from my left.

I whirl around. There, sitting on a blanket under a cherry tree, are the tree man, the tiger, and to my alarm, Étienne. His presence distracts me from myself, so I pray for strength and guidance.

While I stand frozen in place, the tree man repeats, "Are you hungry?"

"Yes, I am." On every level, I add silently.

"Well then, come join us," he says.

Holding my head high to mask my fear, I move toward the blanket, uncertain of how to address Étienne. I think back on my visits with Mary, Isis, and Tonantzin, and connect with the feminine power within me. At last I find the courage to face him.

"Hey, I missed you guys," I remark.

They make room for me on the blanket. I sit by the tiger and look into his friendly eyes. Then I stroke his fur, trying to set my nervous hands at ease. He doesn't seem to mind. The tree man's eyes are twinkling as usual, though I cannot tell if he is laughing at me or with me. My insecurity really mounts when I meet Étienne's gaze. We lock eyes for a moment, then breaking the silence, we say simultaneously, "I'm sorry."

I look down, for my eyes are starting to burn and I do not want to cry. After a moment I am able to face him again. My eyes are watery, but at least no tears are streaming down my cheeks.

Étienne's face softens to meet my vulnerability. "Listen, I felt threatened by our connection. I shouldn't have acted so coldly. I'd like to try our last conversation again."

Our last conversation seems like lifetimes ago, I think to myself. I am in such a different place from when we parted. Isis helped me understand that I don't need this man, that I'm capable of finding happiness without him.

"I've experienced a lot since I last saw you," I reply. "I am ready to start our conversation again. I think I can act differently this time. I have surrendered my desires to the powers that be. I no longer know what is best for us, and I have no intention of trying to hang on to you."

The tree man and the tiger are listening with rapt attention. I am glad Étienne has met my friends, and I am comforted by their presence.

"I need time to sort things out," Étienne continues. "I do have obligations, especially when it comes to following my path. But I don't want to give you up. Part of my learning has to do with being fully present in a relationship. I need some time though, C. I hope you understand."

"I do understand. I don't know if a relationship fits into my life at the moment, although I am certain there is much to be gained in a conscious one. If we are meant to experience that together, it will happen in its own time. I will not fight against the current of life that carries me."

"Congratulations," the tree man says to us. "I think you are both on your way to learning how to support each other while coming home to yourselves. That is what true love is about."

What profound words these are, I observe. I'd like a relationship based on supporting each other in coming home to oneself. I don't want to be in a needy relationship; I want to support Étienne as he strives to come into his power and I want that same support for myself. May it be so.

THE FOUR OF US REMAIN UNDER THE CHERRY TREE ENJOYING the day and the good company. After a while, Étienne and I recount our experiences since our last meeting. His time—taken up by meditation and observation—seems less dramatic than mine, though he did contemplate our relationship.

I continue on eagerly, aware that the tree man and the tiger already know of my impressions but are nonetheless willing listeners. "Partnership with nature, with other humans, and with my true love is a thread that weaves throughout my adventures. The world I come from, on the other hand, is rife with societal breakdown. Apart from times of war or natural disaster, people rarely bond together to share resources or support one another. At one time in our history, the young helped the elders and the elders guided the young, but today these two age groups have little understanding of each other and precious little contact. Families are so spread out that they hardly ever live together as tribes or clans. And although modern medicine has devised extraordinary measures to extend the human life span, it does not assist elders in carrying on with their lives.

"The elders have lost their souls and their visions. Because of this, they can no longer help the young remember who they are and where they come from. Many people in my culture don't even know their ancestral roots.

"To top it off, communities are changing rapidly. The isolation people feel is devastating. Desperate for camaraderie, many teens are joining gangs and acting out in nonproductive ways. And people of all ages are becoming more divisive and self-centered. It seems that we must at least learn to share resources. After all, we share the planet."

The tree man breaks in. "What I am hearing behind your words is an intense level of fear."

"That's true," I reply. "Many people of my time live in fear. Most of my own decisions are sparked by fear. I am hoping to combat some of this anxiety by bridging what I have learned in these worlds with what I know on my own. Some portion of me is now certain that we are all part of a large interconnected web."

"Do you know the cause of this fear you speak of?" the tree man asks. "Central to the theory of evolution is the survival of the fittest. Simply put, your ancestors passed down very strong genes to help you survive. Had you not received this genetic encoding, you would not be here today. Your ancestors endured wars, famines, and other disasters, and their survival instincts have been passed on to you as a knowing. With it has come the message that the species must survive at all costs. Considering this, I'd say that the fear you refer to is a fear of death, a fear that the species will not survive. So it seems that both the fear and the underlying message live within your cells.

"All life forms carry this encoding, for it is part of the earth experience. In addition, all life forms are 'wired' for the fight-or-flight reflex to ensure their survival. So while your connection to nature helps you experience its beauty and its gifts, this connection also guarantees that you will hold the fear of destruction in the cells of your body. As long as you live on earth you will experience fear."

To this I reply, "Much of what you say contradicts what I have been learning on my travels. On the one hand, I am told that I am spirit and cannot be destroyed, that I must give in to the currents of life, that I need to live in harmony. On the other, I am told that fear and the flight-or-flight response are embedded in my cells, enabling the continuation of my ancestral line. How do I live as a spiritual person and a fear-based organism at the same time?"

Étienne, with a gleam in his eye, pipes in, "This is exactly what I have been studying. As long as we are human, we will have a body that reacts with fear. Yet we are not just a body; we are spirit in a body. Hence we can learn to detach from the physical organism. And once detached, we can learn to objectively watch our fear, at which point it no longer runs us. I practice observation, and it has taught me a different response to fear."

"So, what you are all saying is that my fear is natural. It's my *response* to it that needs to change."

"Exactly," Étienne and the tree man answer together. Even the tiger lifts his head in affirmation.

"This is going to take a great deal of practice."

"That's true," replies Étienne. "But you can fashion the tools you'll need to do it. One good approach is to develop a daily exercise of remembering who you are and detaching from the struggle."

"Considering all the information I am gathering here, I definitely have a lot of work to do."

"I need to be honest with you, C. This raises a concern for me," says Étienne. "From what you have shared of your adventures, it seems we are on somewhat different paths. My life is one of contemplation and observation; I am not trying to change the world. If I am to explore a deep relationship with you, I want you to be present in it."

"I don't know how to respond, Étienne. I am simply gathering information and experiences. I don't know how I will bring them into my day-to-day life."

"May I interrupt?" It is the voice of a stranger.

Étienne and I have been so engaged in conversation that we did not notice the approach of the teacher I met after leaving the hospital. I look up at her, suddenly aware that I have never before seen her in daylight. She looks strangely familiar to me.

"My name is Cassandra," she says to Étienne, after which she nods a greeting to me. "May I sit down?"

We make room for her on the blanket. As soon as she has settled in, the tiger moves to her side. She strokes him lovingly, as if she already knows him. The way she meets the gaze of the tree man suggests that they, too, know each other.

Cassandra looks at me and says, "Étienne has shared very important information with you. As you have discovered, each person has a reason for being in life. Part of what will give you meaning in life is participation in a strong, committed relationship. In relationship you will remember who you really are and you will get back in touch with your feminine essence. Yes, you will have work to do in the world, but you must balance this work with feeding and taking care of yourself.

"The time of sacrificing yourself for the good of the whole is over. The goddess will not support martyrdom. So yes, you will have work to do in the world, but you must also continue to work on yourself and to develop whatever it is that you are passionate about. You will learn much from your relationship with Étienne, provided that you commit to it as fully as you have committed to your decision to live. You must walk a path of balance."

"I have received so many messages in the time I have been here. I need to go home and put them into practice before I can wholeheartedly agree with any of them."

"That's true, C," says Cassandra. "Your time of traveling in these worlds will soon end, but you will want to get clear on your priorities before returning home. You will have plenty of time to practice what you have learned, which is what your soul has asked for. Surrender to your soul's journey in these lands. And try not to worry about how you will implement every lesson you have learned here.

"Before you and Étienne part again, you must decide if you want to fully commit to a path of exploring true love. Ask your heart to respond to Étienne's concerns."

"Étienne," I say to him, "I truly do want to commit to you. But you will have to be patient with me. This is all so new."

"I know it is, C. And the thought of committing to you is new for me. I may appear to be in touch with my needs, but perhaps I only think I am. I still have some business to take care of, so why don't we part for now, finish our travels here, and meet again later."

"But how will I find you?"

"Don't worry, *I* will find *you*. You must trust in us and in our love."

"Étienne is right," says Cassandra. The tree man nods in agreement.

"Come walk with me, C," Étienne proposes.

He leads me into the castle through the side door. As we walk down the hallway I remember so well, he seems wrapped in thought.

"What are you thinking about?" I ask.

"I'm trying to decide which room to take you to. I know," he says, stopping in his tracks. "Follow me."

After passing about twenty rooms, he opens the door to one almost at the end of the hall. Although I yearn to explore all the rooms in the castle, my body leads me on. I am more interested in what Étienne has in store than in embarking on new adventures of my own.

At the doorway he takes my hand and looks deep into my eyes, touching all the closed spaces within me. It's as though lights have been turned on in uninhabited rooms. He reaches around and lifts me up. I feel surprisingly light in his embrace.

Crossing the threshold in Étienne's arms, I notice hundreds of white candles lighting this otherwise dark room. In its center is a large wooden bed. Étienne places me gently on the mattress. My body is on fire as he lies down beside me. We kiss passionately, whereupon my fears dissolve and I am once again possessed by the goddess within me. Étienne gently removes my clothes, all the while staring at my body. I do not feel self-conscious. Indeed, the feminine part of me feels secure and burns with desire for him. I sit up and lift his shirt over his head, then he takes off the rest of his clothes.

Lying skin against skin, we become one soul reunited at last. The split will be healed, I tell myself before drifting off to sleep. We spend the night together in an ecstatic embrace.

I awake to gentle streams of light filtering in through the narrow window of the room. The candles have all burned down. I look over to see the soft gaze of Étienne as he awakens. He reaches for me and I snuggle against his body.

"I love you," he whispers into my ear.

"I love you, too," I say, turning to kiss his lips.

"You know, we will be together, C."

"I know. I trust that we will."

"I need to go now. But I will find you, I promise. Do you believe me?"

"I know on a deep level that you will find me, Étienne. My body says that you are telling me the truth. I will miss you terribly, and I will hold you close to my heart."

Étienne kisses me gently on my lips and forehead. Then he jumps out of bed and reaches for his clothes.

"Now, don't follow me this time. You have other places to go, and I'll see you soon. Good journeys!"

Before I am able to respond, he is out the door. Part of me is excited about my future with Étienne. Another part, however, is terrified. There goes that survival instinct, I tell myself. Doesn't it know anything but fear? The need to feel safe and secure has dominated my life. I hope I can find a way to change the program.

I slowly put on my clothes. Stepping into my shoes, I look around the room. The bed is made of dark cherry wood. The walls are also dark, though more likely oak. Covering the narrow window are white lace curtains. The only other object in the room is its mirror, a doorway to another realm. I look into the glass wondering which world it leads to.

Before leaving the room, I take a final look at the bed that held the ecstasy of our union. I feel as if I am taking a mental photo to refer to in the future, while recapturing special moments of my life. Then I step into the hall, shutting the door behind me.

As I stroll down the long passageway, I stop scrutinizing the surroundings. My eyes have turned inward to savor the remnants of the intense love I have shared.

While exiting through the front door of the castle, I spot the little tree man and the tiger waiting for me. Cassandra, it seems, has left.

The three of us begin the long trek back to the meadow. We walk in silence, which allows me to tune into the waves of ecstasy still rolling through my body. Just beyond the manicured lawn, I turn around for one last glimpse at the castle and see it dissolving into nothingness. Its disappearance does not surprise me, for I realize that although the passion occurring there felt real, the castle itself never did.

We continue on, watching the changing angles of light as the sun passes across the sky. When we approach the cave of crystals, the tiger stops and offers his back to ride upon. The tree man and I climb up. The creature's fur tickles my skin, still alive from lovemaking. Squirming around, I search for a comfortable position; and as soon as I settle down, he takes off. The wind slaps against my face, drawing my attention to the elements around me.

We come at last to the tall grasses of the meadow and, yards ahead, an opening in the earth, which I recognize as the place of my arrival. Here the tiger stops, and the tree man and I dismount. As soon as my feet hit the ground, I make my way to the tiger's head and look into his eyes—one blue, the other green. I feel no remorse as I say good-bye to him, because I know we will be friends for a long time. But I do give him a big hug and plant a kiss on his forehead.

The tree man pats the tiger on the head. Afterward, they seem to communicate a silent message to each other.

Turning away, the little man and I enter the dark tunnel. I am surprised to be met by rushing water instead of the cool, dark earth to which I've become accustomed. I swim easily through the narrow tunnel and into the cool waters of the lagoon. Here the setting sun blots out all but the soft outline of the rising full moon. I hear her calling my name and I know I will meet her before returning home. I'm learning to trust my intuition, to believe in what I know to be true.

Swimming to the water's edge, I watch the tree man greet the doe with a kiss on the nose. Then I pull myself out of the lagoon and gaze into the doe's welcoming brown eyes. Looking up at the tops of the pine trees, I sense that my time in this realm has ended. A nod from the tree man confirms my hunch.

"I can't imagine saying good-bye to you," I tell him. "This place feels like home to me. I can come back again, can't I?"

"Yes, of course. This is your home in these worlds, and you will be returning often. We don't need to say good-bye, C."

"I would like to finish my conversation with Isis, but I don't know the way to her dwelling. Can you help me find her again?"

The tree man takes me to a clearing, where he builds a small fire. "Step into the fire. It will help you transform so that you can travel to the home of Isis. Keep her dwelling as your intention, or you may become distracted and end up somewhere else along the way."

The tree man reaches for my hand and gently kisses it. His touch conveys his message: Good-bye for now.

I gaze into his smiling eyes, my heart filled full with love for him. Amid all the beautiful spirits I have met, I realize, none has touched my heart and soul the way he has. Never before have I experienced the depth of love I feel between us.

Then, with some sadness in my heart, I step into the fire and turn to smoke. My spirit melds with the spirit of fire, and I soar into the far reaches of the universe.

ONCE AMID THE CLOUDS, I FEEL MY BODY STARTING TO RE-form. My intention does indeed keep me traveling to the home of Isis—so much so that I do not even glance at the passing landscapes. At last I begin to slow down, aware that I am reaching my destination. I stop at the simple, sacred, open-air home beside the Nile.

Isis, sitting on the floor weaving a basket, looks up at me and smiles.

I step inside to greet her. "It's good to be back here with you."

"You have wasted no time during your travels—you are on quite a mission. Please have a seat."

I sit on the woven rug. "You live in such a beautiful home. There's something special about the energy it radiates."

"This house has much soul. Everything you see in it has special meaning to me. Many of these items I have made."

"My living quarters lack vitality. I wonder how I might bring the sacred to my apartment."

"The answer draws upon some of the information you received from my sister Tonantzin. What you are really saying is that you want your home, your sacred space, to mirror your own soulfulness, or life force. When you look about, you want to see a space that reflects back vitality.

"Just as you have a soul, so does the land on which you live and the structure in which you reside. But because the essence in all things animate or inanimate is not honored in your time, you are surrounded by lifelessness. Actually, there are many ways to bring the soul back to your dwelling. You can ask it to return, for example. Or you can sing it back. I like to sing, so that is my way.

"Once you have called back the soul of your dwelling, you can bring in objects that hold power for you, that seem alive. Rocks or fresh flowers will do the trick. Whatever object you decide upon, try raising your awareness of it by asking: What part of me does this object mirror back? Does it hold power and life for me? If it does not, don't place it in your home. As for the items already present, decide which ones you want to keep and which ones you need to let go of.

"You can sanctify every room in your home, or you may prefer to designate one room as sacred space. The point is to love and appreciate the place in which you live. All souls want appreciation, even those inhabiting our homes.

"This holds true for your office as well. You can place on your desk a special object, like a crystal, flower, or stone that will change the energy of your workplace. Remember, life can exist everywhere, even beneath artificial lighting. You just have to call it in.

"There is no right way to do this, so experiment. Notice whether you feel a positive shift in energy after bringing in a new object. If you do, you'll know your work has been successful. If you don't, you'll know you have more work to do."

"Thank you for your suggestions," I say, fascinated by these notions.

"Let's take a walk," Isis suggests, standing up and heading out the door.

Before leaving, I take in the splendor of her home. The "soul of a place" is an intriguing concept, I note, vowing to inhabit a space that encompasses as much life force and good energy as I feel here.

I follow Isis through the grasslands in the valley of the Nile. The grasses here, although beautiful, are not as soft and lush as those in the meadow.

"Each place I have visited in these worlds has a unique beauty and energy, Isis," I tell her.

"I'm sure you can say that about each being you have met, too," she replies.

"That's definitely true. I have been introduced to some extraordinary energies."

"You will also find this to be true of each human being you meet. Every person is born with a unique beauty and essence. To compare one with another would be impossible, yet this is what your culture attempts to do. People are classified by race, status, and education, instead of being recognized for the energy they carry. This impersonal treatment has been catastrophic, has it not?"

"Of course it has. You need not say more."

"All that is unique about each person has been lost. What has replaced the understanding of your true essence is the definition of yourself that your parents, teachers, and other authority figures gave you. These definitions have led to a false identity. Moreover, they have prohibited you from living up to your full potential, from living out your birthright. Your birthright is to fully express your soul.

"You have learned a great deal about yourself in these worlds. You experienced your true origins. You explored your fears. You saw how you've stepped out of the rhythms of nature. You discovered some of the work you are to do. Now you must dissociate from the voices that block you from being who you really are. You must learn to go beyond your social conditioning."

Isis stops walking and mounts a large rock. I take a seat on the ground beside her. The singsong quality of her voice reminds me of the attendant in the hospital at the beginning of my travels. I am captivated by these hypnotic tones, for they are in perfect harmony with her energy.

I sit with my arms around my knees looking up into her jet-black eyes, eager to hear more.

"Can you tell the difference between hearing something that is true and hearing a lie?" she inquires.

"Actually, I can," I reply. "I have always thought I had a built-in lie detector. When I know something is true, I often see a green light flashing in my solar plexus. When I think someone has told a lie, or when I am about to make a wrong decision, I see a red flag. I don't always heed these signals, but I do get them."

"That's good—it's a start. As you embark on a path of right action, listen to the voices in your mind. Each time you hear one, ask yourself, 'Is this me speaking or someone from my past?' If it is you, seek out the information it holds. If it is someone else, try to identify the speaker and let the message go.

"The better you are at sorting out your own voice, the sooner you will get in touch with your true nature. As you have already learned, fears reside within you as part of your genetic code. Your job is to thank them for their assistance in sustaining you, then detach from them and go to a deeper, all-knowing part of yourself—the part you think of as the observer. From this place you will be able to access the fountain of light within you. Energy will come from this light; passion will come from this light; creativity will come from this light. The feminine part of you will experience this energy, and the male, or dynamic, part of you will help manifest it in the world."

"But how much of my past do I need to know? How seriously must I look at what went wrong?"

"You need to look at your past hurts and mistakes to determine what you want to change. You need to be aware that your past hurts have developed voices that keep you from being who you really are. But it is nonproductive to get lost in your past, for there is no freedom in analyzing and reanalyzing prior events. Freedom arises in finding out why you are here and who you are beyond your conditioning.

"You have choices as an adult that you did not have as a child. How freeing it is to know that you are not locked in to your past! If you get lost in your wounds and fail to see your current options, you will only re-create the wounding."

"I understand what you are saying. I have avoided looking at my past for reasons that I now know are unimportant. Yes, I can see the benefit in looking back so I can decide on the changes to make in my life. But I can't figure out what has meaning for me and why I am here, other than to shine. I wish I had a bit more direction on this assignment."

"To find one's life purpose, one can go on a quest for a vision or seek the answer in a dream. Many spiritual practices can also help access this information. The journey you have embarked upon will assist you, and will continue over time.

"Here is another technique that may come in handy: Try to ascertain exactly what nourishes you on all levels, including the physical. Remember that although you may not be a body, your body carries your spirit and must therefore be tended to. While preparing meals, pour love into them. While selecting foods to eat, ask yourself if they will nourish you. Check in to see whether or not particular actions will nourish you. *Only partake in what is nourishing.*"

"A lot of work is involved in taking personal responsibility for one's life," I comment.

"It's not as hard as coping with the consequences of not taking responsibility," Isis remarks. "Your task will be eased by all that you learn on your on your travels as well as in your relationship with Étienne. Your relationship with him will be a true creation story. You will also begin to seek out like-minded people with whom you will share a variety of resources.

"C, you will be an instrument for the goddess. And remember, an instrument must allow itself to be played. It cannot play itself."

Nourished by her words, I say, "The teachers I have met in these worlds often talk about the cycles and rhythms of nature. Is there more you can tell me about this?"

"Oh, you are about to meet your greatest teacher. Let her show you the way."

With this, Isis slides off the rock and declares, "Come, I will take you to her."

THE MOON IS RISING AS ISIS LEADS ME TO THE NILE. BY THE riverbank, she lifts her arms and a strong wind comes up.

"Accept help from the wind spirit," she instructs.

I plant my feet on the ground, about a shoulder-width apart, and turn my hands palms up at my sides. The wind is so strong that I am forced to shut my eyes. It rips away at my body, whereupon my skin, my bones, every bit of matter dissolves to sand. As sand, I am picked up by another gust of wind.

Then, in the same way an hourglass siphons its contents into the lower portion of the vessel, I am siphoned back into my body. Wiggling my toes, I feel granular particles beneath them. My nose picks up the salty, algae infused scent of the sea. My ears open to the roar of waves.

Lifting my eyelids, still slightly stuck together with sand, I find myself on a beach facing an immense ocean in the midst of the night. Directly above me is the moon, which has begun waning. I am transfixed watching her reflection in the water. I recall that I have often imagined myself alone on a beach watching the reflection of the moon in the water. My mind fills with recollections of the many times I heard the moon calling me during my travels and with my recurring quandary about how to answer her call.

Delighted to be face-to-face with her shining beauty, I sit with my legs crossed and my hands, palms up, resting on my knees. Closing my eyes, I become bathed in moonbeams. The light swirling through my body is nothing like sunlight, which feeds my cells; this light nourishes my soul and takes me to the core of my being.

Allowing myself to be nurtured by the light of the moon, the sound of the waves, and the smell of the sea, I become immersed in memories . . . I grew up by the sea, dancing in her waves and being dragged into her currents. Sometimes I felt as if she would never let me loose, as if she'd take me out to her home to live with her forever. But each time I tumbled into her embrace, she would spit me out before it was too late.

I never feared the sea. In fact, I floated endlessly on her surface, watching the clouds drift by and cherishing the way she rocked me. Even when I was in pain I'd go to her. Her rolling waves would pull my sorrows from me, recharging me with new life on their return. The sea was always there to love me when I had no one to share my sadness with.

Breathing in tempo with the undulant waves, I once again feel the healing action of the sea as she takes away what needs to be released and brings in fresh energy. No longer do I yearn to communicate with her, except to express my appreciation for her regenerative presence in my life. I take a moment to give her thanks.

Then I gaze up at the moon, wondering how to contact her. At that moment I hear a voice. "Do you remember when you were a child, C, and went outside every night to sing a song of love and praise to the man in the moon?"

"I have forgotten about that."

"Well, I haven't. You sang to me with an open heart,

calling me into your life forever. And like a guardian angel, I have been watching over you for many years. Now it is time for you to learn my mysteries. It is good that you have come when I've begun to wane."

"Why is that?" I ask.

"I reveal my mysteries while waning. When I am waxing, the light of the sun blots out my essence. Only when I cease to reflect the sun's rays can I show my true nature."

She adds, "Close your eyes and allow me to create a space in which you can experience your own fullness."

I close my eyes. Beams of light enfold me as tenderly as loving arms. Wrapped in her embrace, I drop deep inside myself and begin to see her light reflected in me. Her light soon fills me completely.

"Your concentration is good. I can tell that you are in an expanded state."

She's right—I have surrendered to her and, in the process, relinquished all ties to my body. I am in a state of pure beingness.

"Isn't the silence wonderful?" she asks.

The absence of noise within me is so profound I don't want to disrupt it. But awareness starts to creep in. I am slowly becoming conscious of myself.

The moon says, "Awareness causes the expansion to collapse, doesn't it?"

"Yes, I feel like a balloon losing its air."

"Awareness of self ushers in the state of separateness. When you become aware of yourself, you perceive the illusion of disconnectedness from the All."

The ensuing silence leaves me to my thoughts. Humans have evolved into self-aware beings. This self-awareness can be a gift, yet it can also be a curse, especially when under the rule of the ego we forget the web of life we are a part of.

The moon breaks my train of thought. "Look into me and see the reflection of your life on earth and your journeys in these worlds."

As I look into the face of the moon, I see a movie screen and upon it a film that unfolds in full color. I see my birth and watch myself as a young child on a chaise lounge singing to the moon. I see happy scenes in which I was still connected to nature and experiencing the love and care of my parents. I then see myself becoming socialized, all the while losing bits and pieces of my essence. My creative fire leaves when I am a schoolgirl being molded to conform to the rules and norms of society.

I see family members, teachers, other authority figures, friends, and strangers, all throwing clay onto the sculpture that is me. They fling out their projections, beliefs, attitudes, judgments, and feelings. Before long I have lost my identity to the figurine forged by others.

I watch the clay begin to harden, wearing on my body and creating an unnatural tension. I am weighted down by the rules of society, the projections cast by others, and the negative feelings in the world around me.

I watch as the stresses I put myself through cause my body to crack, whereupon illness flows into me. While I remain separated from my true self, the illness takes up residence in my body, the container of my spirit. But some part of my being, determined to survive, creates a crisis that opens doors to other realms, where I am encouraged to remember who I am.

More scenes unfold—meetings with the tree man and the doe, the tiger, the skeleton, the anaconda, Cassandra, Our Lady of Guadalupe, Mary, Isis, Tonantzin, and Lao-tzu. I watch Jonathan and Leah showing me the baskets of lights waiting excitedly to be born.

I see my birth, my soul retrieval, my recommitment to

life, and my romance with Étienne. And I see the moon showering me with her light.

I merge with the moon. Inhaling, I feel a pull; exhaling, a release. The earth and the moon, I now know, breathe as one. The tides of the oceans are ruled by her, as are the growth cycles of plants and the biological rhythms of animals and humans. All living beings grow, act, and react in accordance with her changes.

"I have a great deal to teach you," the moon says, blending her voice into my reverie. "What you are learning tonight is only a beginning. Do you understand?"

"Yes, I will come to you when I can."

"I have great patience. You have already sensed the power of my magnetism and you have learned from others that what exists outside you and within you are one and the same."

Taking her words deep inside me, I nod in agreement.

"Among the governing principles of the universe are laws of attraction that determine what you draw into your life. While inhaling, you call to yourself your intention to live, and then find inside what wants to be created. While exhaling, you 'breathe out' your creation thoughts to the universe. The universe hears these and responds by bringing you the vibration you have sent out.

"You see, all thoughts have a vibration. Positive and negative thoughts vibrate differently, calling forth different situations. Would you like to see how this works?"

"Yes, of course," I reply.

"Closing your eyes, think about Étienne and your new love for him. Experience a smile forming in your heart."

"I can do that."

"Now open your heart and ask to be shown the vibration of your love."

"When I see the vibration, it looks like small pink

bubbles. When I listen, it sounds similar to the humming of the attendant I first met in the hospital and to the voice of Isis."

I momentarily allow myself to be distracted by the roar of the waves hitting the shore as the tide rolls in.

"Now let's try something else. Think about a person who evokes anger within you."

"I would rather not call in that energy right now."

"Do it for a learning. Humor me."

I go inside myself and think of someone toward whom I project strong negativity. I feel the beast of anger waking up and rising within me.

"The sound emanating from my being is discordant, and the darkness around me is nothing like the purity of the night sky."

"You can imagine what you will get when *this* call is answered."

"Yes," I say, opening my eyes to disrupt the imagery. I let the energy from the waves wash over me, clearing the negativity that has arisen.

"When you put out negative thoughts, beliefs, and attitudes, or even engage in negative daydreaming, you run the risk of attracting problematic situations."

"But I can't always control the thoughts I have."

"That's true—you cannot kill your shadow. But you can raise your awareness to grasp the source of problematic states of consciousness. You move into these states when you become disconnected from the fountain of light within you. Each time you are pulled from your center you experience dissonance, breathing out discordant notes into the universe. Those notes are then mirrored back into your life.

"Awareness without judgment is the key. Investigate the source of disharmony within you. Are you hearing your own voice or one from your past? Can you return to center after you have been pulled out by the energy of another's voice?"

"What if I can't identify the voice, or can't find my way back to center? Am I doomed to suffer the consequences?"

"I see no doom in your life. But you will not always be able to identify the source of your emotions and thoughts. Sometimes, an energy inside you will spark feelings while breaking loose at the end of its life span. Other times, a body organ processing toxins will trigger a variety of emotions. All these sensations will ride themselves out. Nor will you always be able to stop your thoughts, although you can learn to harness their energy and work with it. You can learn to transmute negative thought forms into energy that is beneficial for yourself and others. Remember, energy that is transformed converts to power.

"On some occasions, you will call forth a drama to reenact so you can learn a particular lesson. When this occurs, simply remind yourself that you are an actor in a play. Receive the lesson, then shed your costume.

"On other occasions, you will create a drama to awaken yourself to a belief or emotion brooding within you. This, too, is a learning and a gift, for the more conscious you are of your shadow, the less likely it is to play itself out in your psyche, catching you off guard."

I look up. The stars are beginning to fade and the sky is turning from black to blue.

"Can you give me an example of this?" I ask, lifting my knees from the sand and wrapping my arms around them.

"Let's take your relationship with Étienne. You were not aware that you called out to the universe for true love, were you?"

"No, you're right about that."

"Then you were probably not aware of a belief you held—namely, that you do not deserve love. If you don't

bring this belief fully into consciousness, you might manifest it in your waking life."

"So, what you are saying is that I need to develop a
practice."

"Yes, living life consciously is a practice, my dear."

Even the ocean falls silent in response to these words.

"You reminded me that when I was a child I sang to
you, thinking you were the man in the moon. I now experience you as feminine. What are you really?"

"I am both male and female, for I embrace all. You,
like others, see what you need to see in order to learn
what you need to learn. Some peoples of the earth have
named me Grandfather Moon; others call me Grandmother Moon. I am both. I reveal myself in whatever way is
needed."

"Tonantzin told me that men and women alike need
to get in touch with their feminine aspects. I suppose this
is true for me as well."

"Yes, you must heal the male-female split within you.
The male dynamic in you is trying to oppress the more
intuitive female essence. Why? Because it feels threatened by your rising feminine power. Instead, a strong
partnership must be created. The male in you needs the
female as a receiver of information. The female in you
needs the dynamism of the action-oriented male. You
will heal this split in the context of your relationship with
Étienne."

"Healing a split of this magnitude will probably
require much creativity. But I often feel disconnected
from my power—or as you put it, my fountain of light."

"There is an ebb and flow to life. When you are in the
ebb, you forget that the flow will be coming back around.
When you are in the flow, you fear the ebb. The best
approach is to stay in the present. Life will bring changes
soon enough.

"Your creative power, by the way, comes with the waning moon. Did you know that?"

"I'm afraid I have not been following your cycles."

"Your ancestors did."

"I know little about my ancestors. Their customs were not passed down to me."

"You would find it most fruitful to explore your ancestry. If you can acquire a sense of your past, you will have a better understanding of your present. You will even be able to trace this energy into the future. You will then be equipped to view life as a continuum.

"Your ancestors possessed talents and strengths that have been passed on to you. Honor them by trying to retrieve this information. It is part of the foundation they've laid for your life."

"I have been told that you will teach me about the cycles of nature," I state, aware that the sky is lightening and that my time with this great presence is coming to an end.

"I will teach you more about nature's rhythms after you complete this assignment: Follow my cycles, noting the shifts in your energy and disposition. Observe how your own cycles change relative to mine. Watch how the growth and dormancy phases of plants correspond to my cycles. Notice how the animals scurry about and rest in keeping with my cycles.

"As you do this, take note of the changes you feel through the passing seasons. Observe how each one alters the quality of energy available to you. Notice when you feel the need to pull in and when you desire the company of others.

"The wind changes with each season, as does the temperature, the humidity, the scent in the air. The colors of the sky as well as the positions of the sun and moon change, too. Learn to conduct your life without a

calendar. Use the elements you see, feel, smell, and hear to inform you of the seasons.

"The stress you create by being out of sync with the earth's rhythms is a major cause of disease in your time. You cannot control nature, for nature controls you. So relax into the rhythmic breathing of the earth. Take note of all this, then return to tell me what you have learned. On that night I will teach you more."

The beams of light that have been embracing me withdraw into the early morning sky. Venus, the morning star, rises and sits by the moon.

I honor the ocean and the moon, and they honor me. I feel them entering me from under my ribs and taking their rightful places within me. The moon rises toward my forehead, to a spot above and between my eyes. The ocean rolls into my heart. When they reach their dwelling places, they share their power with me.

"May I sit with you?"

Recognizing this voice, I turn around. "Of course, Cassandra," I say.

"You've had many travels, and it is time to go home," she acknowledges, taking a seat beside me. "How do you feel about this?"

I gaze at the two celestial bodies just above the horizon. "I feel ready, and at the same time I am afraid. There is so much information to bridge into my life. I know the way will be shown to me if I keep my heart open. I guess I fear the unknown."

"Fear of the unknown is natural. It will keep you humble. But remember, life is an adventure—so set your sights on the adventure and let some of your fear transform into excitement, into the thrill of meeting the unknown.

"As you have already been told, many seen and unseen forces will be on hand to help. And you will continue to visit the beings you have encountered, each one of whom will assist you in your learning."

I take comfort in Cassandra's presence. Because she met me at the beginning of my journey, her appearance at its end comes as no surprise. I look up into her face and peer into her eyes. Something about her is oddly familiar. Suddenly I realize that she looks like an older version of me. My eyes widen with amazement.

"That's right, C. Even the energy of your future is on hand to help. Go now in peace," she says, gently pulling me to my feet.

The wind that brought me here returns, blowing through my hair and my clothes. Dissolving into sand once again, I move toward a tunnel of muted light extending from the sky. As soon as I step inside, I begin to re-form. I climb up through the tunnel until I arrive at a misty doorway.

Lao-tzu, holding his curved staff, waits for me in the fog. "The river of life will lead you to paradise if you stay true to it," he whispers, leaning over and kissing me on the forehead. Then he steps aside, clearing the way to my passage back home.

I AWAKE TO THE DISTANT SOUNDS OF SIRENS BLARING AND THE dazzling gleam of fluorescent lights. Oh my, I think to myself, what a welcome home!

A nurse dressed in a white uniform gazes kindly upon me and says, "There was quite a commotion during your surgery—an earthquake rocked the hospital and damaged some of our equipment. You have been in and out of a coma for the past two weeks. Now, however, you are fine. Let me get the surgeon for you."

As she turns to leave, I become aware of my body. It feels stiff and bruised. I am in pain, but mostly I am groggy. Little by little, memories surface and push away the fog. Then fear and excitement bubble up as I remember my mission in life.

The door swings open and in walks the doctor, reading my chart. He peers at me over the top of his glasses, then clears his throat.

"I have some good news for you. When we opened you up, there was no tumor to be found. This sometimes happens, though I cannot explain why. Just feel lucky."

Embracing the love and compassion of all the beings I have left behind, I say, "I do. I feel most blessed. I give thanks for my life."

Taken aback by my words, he wishes me luck and turns to leave. As he opens the door, I see Étienne standing on the other side of it.

A new adventure awaits.

Dear Reader,

While writing this book, I have been a most fortunate recipient of the kindness, wisdom, and love of the spirits guiding me. The technique I used to access them is referred to as *shamanic journeying,* an ancient visionary method utilized to explore the hidden universe otherwise known primarily through myth and dream. The shamanic journey is used to access spiritual information as well as healing knowledge.

With each push of the pen, I was following my mission to teach through stories based in fiction. I plan to continue following my passion as long as it lasts. A sequel to the adventures of C Alexandra will be released shortly.

With best wishes,

About the Author

Sandra Ingerman, MA, is a world-renowned teacher of shamanism. She is recognized for bridging ancient cross-cultural healing methods into our modern culture, addressing the needs of our times.

A licensed therapist, she is the author of *Soul Retrieval, Welcome Home, A Fall to Grace, Medicine for the Earth: How To Transform Personal and Environmental Toxins, Shamanic Journeying: A Beginner's Guide*, and *How to Heal Toxic Thoughts: Simple Tools for Personal Transformation*. Sandra is also the author of "The Beginner's Guide to Shamanic Journeying", "The Soul Retrieval Journey", and "Miracles for the Earth" lecture programs produced by Sounds True.

Visit www.shamanicvision.com/ingerman.html to read her monthly column The Transmutation News and to read her training schedule.

Visit www.sandraingerman.com to read articles written by Sandra and to see her Training schedule.

Visit www.shamanicteachers.com to find a local teacher or practitioner.

ORDER FORM
Books by Sandra Ingerman

Quantity	Title	Amount
_____	*A Fall to Grace* ($12.00 each)	_____
_____	*Soul Retrieval: Mending the Fragmented Self* ($14.00 each)	_____
_____	*Welcome Home: Following Your Soul's Journey Home* ($14.00 each)	_____
	NM sales tax of 5.75% (for New Mexico residents)	_____
	Shipping and handling (see chart below)	_____
	TOTAL AMOUNT	_____

Discounts available on orders of 10 or more books.

Shipping and Handling

	First Class	Surface
US	$4.00	$2.70
Canada	$4.20	$3.20
Europe	$7.00	$4.00
Australia	$9.00	$5.00

Please add $1.00 per book on orders of two or more.

Method of Payment

❑ Check or money order enclosed (made payable to **Welcome Home,** in US currency only)

❑ MasterCard
❑ VISA

Signature _____

Expiration date

(*Note:* Credit-card charges appearing on your statement will be billed to Welcome Home.)

Please photocopy this order form, fill it out, and mail it, together with your name, address, and personal check, money order, or charge-card information, to:

Moon Tree Rising
p r o d u c t i o n s

PO Box 4757
Santa Fe, NM 87502
888-206-4808